NICHOLAS WARACK

The Sailor & The Porteña

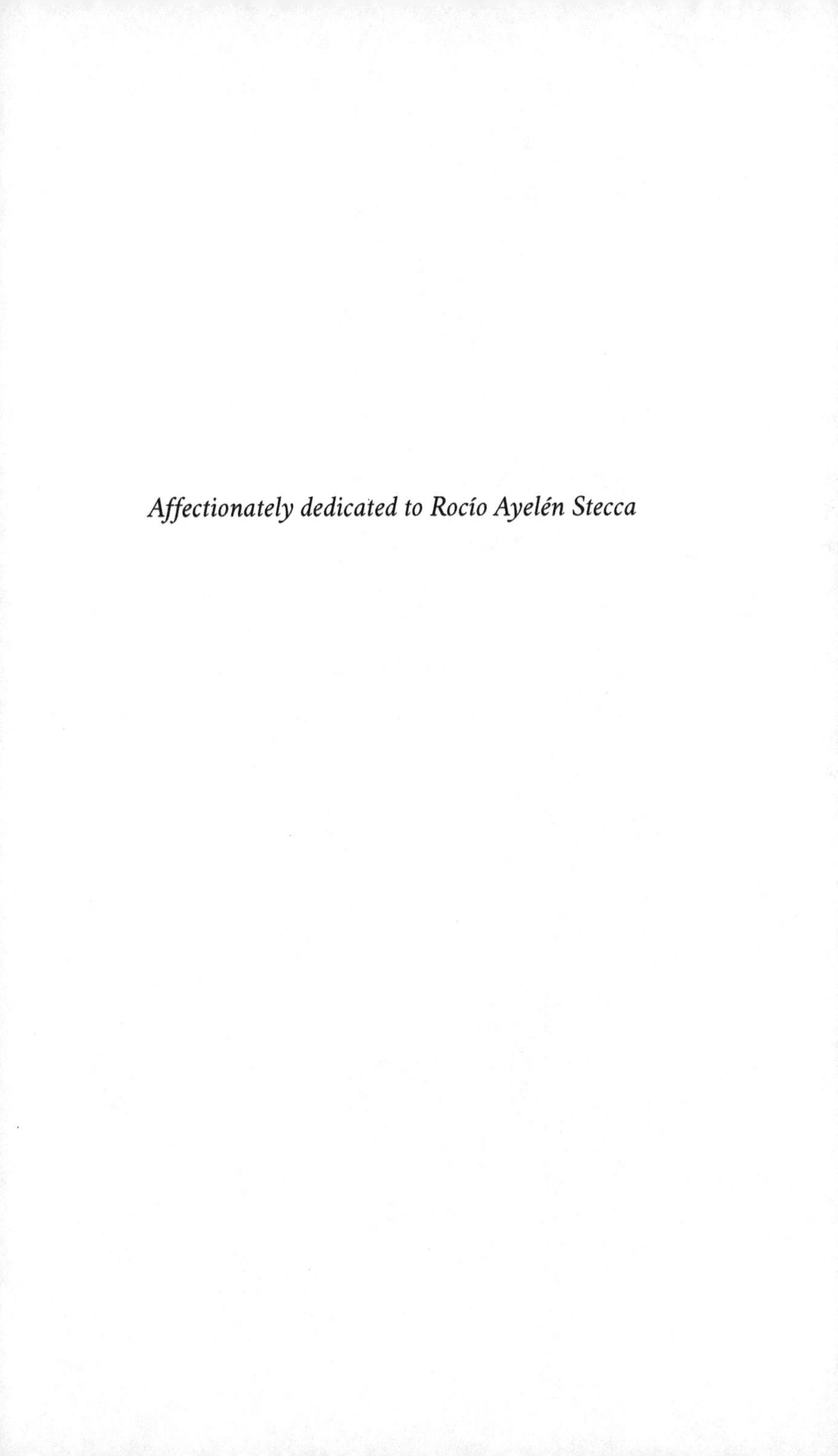

Affectionately dedicated to Rocío Ayelén Stecca

Chapter 1

My car swerved and shimmied back and forth in place, headlights flashing from one side of the crest of the suburban road to the other. Its rear-wheel tires kicked up slush.

"Come on, you ol' hunk o' junk. Put that rubber down!" I ordered my '48 Packard Clipper.

I punched it again with the stick hovering in second gear. The car groaned and rattled, trying in vain to mount the slippery incline. I yanked the wheel, hoping to catch some asphalt, only to push the front wheels over a patch of ice. We descended again.

"No, no, no, no, no!"

The car came to rest at the foot of the hill with a metallic whine. I slammed my palm into the steering wheel and sat back in the seat. The Clipper puttered like an affable mutt, waiting for someone to throw the stick again. I was not going to make it home tonight, and I was tired—plum tired. I usually was, but this was the kind of tired that deadened the senses. I was pulling extra shifts at the factory and hadn't thought much about the snowstorm coming through. Foolish on my part, but it wasn't any good to mope now, I thought. I took a gander around me. These hilly neighborhoods in Greater Pittsburgh all looked the same—lines of brick and wood construction—but I recognized this particular one. It was the hill a block down from my grandparents' house. I remembered sledding down this steep street as a boy when I would visit the house with Mom and Dad. I didn't normally drive this way to my place, but whenever we had this kind of weather, the traffic would get so backed up on the main roads you nearly froze to death waiting. I thought the detour would save me the trouble, but there I was, stuck at the bottom of a hill.

Quiet folks, my grandparents were. I never gave them much thought before that night. They were more or less as boring as other folks' grandparents, I supposed. They had never asked much of me, and I hadn't seen them a lot since I got back from serving in Korea.

"Hell," I said to no one.

I put the car in reverse, managed to park it along the sidewalk, and cut the engine. I stepped out. It was damn cold, the kind that stings the lungs. I tossed my coat on over my coveralls and jogged up the street. I wandered past the plain ol' houses until I entered the neighborhood's slightly more affluent section. One could tell by the Victorian fretwork trimming along the ledges and gabled roofs. A little white one with sky-blue shutters sat on a corner intersection. Lights glowed inside, and smoke wafted from its chimney. I came to its door and knocked. The sweet sounds and aromas of hissing beef, bell peppers, eggs, and potatoes carried through the apertures of the home. My reluctance turned to optimism, as I had a sorry pot of oatmeal waiting for me at home. The door opened, and there stood my grandmother.

"Riley!" she said. "What a pleasant surprise! What on earth are you doing here!"

"Hey, Abu," I replied. (I had called my grandma Abu for as long as I could remember, though it was not her name.) Her gray hair was tied beneath a floral headscarf, and she wore a purple apron over a sunflower-colored dress.

"My car broke down," I said. "Would you mind if I stayed here for the night?"

"Why, of course!" she exclaimed. "Come in, Come in! Any grandchild of mine is always welcome. I was just preparing supper." I stepped inside, and she took my jacket and hung it on the coat rack.

"Thank you, Abu."

"Would you care for a cup of coffee? You must be freezing. You haven't eaten yet, have you?"

I'd always found it strange that she prepared coffee so late in the day. Nonetheless, it seemed nice for a cold Friday evening.

"Sure," I replied. "And no. No, I have not."

"Well, good. I'll have supper ready in an hour or so. Why don't you take a seat in the living room with your grandpa?"

"Sure."

I followed her into the kitchen, where she poured a mug of freshly dripped coffee. She then led me to the living room. Grandpa sat asleep in his rocking chair next to the window, where snow piled on the sill. The fireplace crackled, and the adjacent Crosley record player hummed a rockabilly tune at a volume less than Grandpa's snores. Abu reached out a hand to wake him but stopped herself. Instead, she turned to me.

"He sleeps a bit more these days," she said.

"That's fine. I'm happy just to take a load off as well."

"Good," she said, beaming. I'll call for you two shortly."

I nodded again, and she puttered on into the kitchen. I made my way to the couch, to the spot I had made my own so many years before, and set myself down. I looked around at the room, which hadn't changed a bit. I was reminded why I'd barely given this place a thought for years because it seemed there wasn't much to think about here. Abu and Grandpa are my mother's parents, and they talked little about their lives. I knew they had moved around a bit when my mother was a girl before settling here, but she, too, never talked much about it, or maybe I hadn't asked. It was at that moment, for some reason I never quite figured out, that I noticed the blue book across the room.

I had seen it before, embedded in the same spot. Its nameless hardcover spine stared at me—I could feel it—and the sudden urge to enlist its services came over me. I sat up from the couch and tugged it from its crevice on the bookshelf. It was just as blank on its cover as its spine—nothing but buckram and deckled edges. The spine crackled. I stopped and shifted my gaze towards Grandpa. It felt like snoopery, but I had already succumbed to the temptation. He twiddled his whiskers and flexed the age spots on his head but remained sound asleep. I opened it to the title page and read the handwritten words: *The Sailor & The Porteña.*

Chapter 2

The merchant steamship *Dismal Queen* chugged along through the port of Puerto Madero, greeting the docks with two loud drones of her foghorn. A sandy-haired sailor leaned on the starboard side taffrail, his dusky eyes grazing over the city skyline of Buenos Aires. He let his hands drift over the buffed shorthairs around his chin and chops, admiring their sharpness. While the craft wove among the ships, silos, and cranes looming over the narrow waterway of the Río Dique, he marveled at the blend of Renaissance and Neoclassical–style structures that prevailed in the city. Observing their white stone façades, ornate details, and steep glazed roofs, his mind wandered through the city streets below them.

"It's somethin', isn't it, Andrew, ol' boy?" came a chummy voice behind the sailor.

Andrew turned his gaze toward his shipmate, Vincent. He was near the same age as Andrew, but lankier, and often sported an eager smile on his wide lips. He rapped Andrew on the back and then rested his elbows on the railing beside him.

"It is," replied Andrew. "I always look forward to places like this."

Vincent paused to study the passing buildings. "Reminds me

of Paris," he remarked. "And you said much the same when we stopped in Paris … and in Liverpool … Charleston … Cape Town—hell, I don't know a time you didn't say it, for that matter."

Andrew shook his head and smiled. "Another place, another port. As long as we never stay, I'm happy."

Vincent rolled his eyes. "I get it—you were tired of that ol' farm life of yours in Virginia and did what half the dupes on this ship do: sign on with a crew. You do the work, you don't gripe—I give you that—but you're never going to be happy, my friend."

"What are you talking about? This is a good life. I like it."

"You like it because you're always thinkin' there's somethin' new. You're never going to be content."

Andrew scrunched up his face and looked at Vincent. "I'm not following."

"Look," said Vincent condescendingly, "We work, we drink, we make merry without a care in the world—except for yours truly, the salt next to you, and the tub you're on. But, you're still an unfulfilled ol' boy—always thinking there is something better, something different. Let me tell you, the only things that change in this life are ports and harbors. People are all the same: they shit, they die, and somewhere in between, they bitch their way through it. You've got to get what's yours while you can. Enjoy the fruits of your labor—a good woman and a good drink. There isn't much more out there for the likes of us. The sooner you settle your heart with that, the sooner you can stop chasing those dotty dreams of yours. Also, the others won't look at you so funny." He finished with a finger pointed at Andrew.

Andrew dropped his eyes. In some respects, Vincent was

right. Andrew came from a family of sharecroppers in the marshy farmlands of Pungo in the southeastern part of Virginia. Their pride derived from the fact that their sharecropping days had come to an end ten years ago. Andrew's father joined the 34th Virginia Infantry in the War of Succession, as he called it. A few years after he returned, he married Andrew's mother, and she gave birth to Andrew and to two more boys shortly thereafter. Hard times befell the American South in the era of Reconstruction. Many Virginians had little land to call their own, due to devastated markets and capital, relegating them to sharecropping as a means to get by. From the age of five, Andrew and his brothers woke up before dawn to do chores and work until sunset. The family scrimped and saved what they could, hoping to buy the land they worked for.

Little good it did, for every dollar saved was every dollar spent. In their hearts, the family knew this venture was all for naught, but such a sweet lie made watery soups and stale bread go down better than a bitter truth. Hope arrived when Andrew's grandfather passed. His assets fell to his wife, and because of her frail state, Andrew's parents took her in under the condition she would bequeath the inheritance to Andrew's father. She moved in, and Andrew's father finally possessed the deed to the land they thought he would never have.

Everything changed that day. Andrew's father welded his identity to his sovereignty. Every soul who crossed his path endured his sermons about toil and strife that had been cultivated into deserved glory and riches. He generally prologued these sermons with quotations that smacked of the pulpit, citing his favorites: Proverbs 21:5 ("The thoughts of the diligent tend only to plenteousness; but of everyone that is hasty only to want.") or 12:24 ("The hand of the diligent shall bear rule; but the slothful shall be under tribute."). His ego's contrived importance had elevated him to the status of a landowner equal to that of the planter class of old. For seven years, he sat in his rocking chair—coffee in the morning, beer in the afternoon—shouting his displeasure and making empty threats at his laboring progeny, especially Andrew. As the eldest son, Andrew was expected to take the lion's share of the work from which his father had divested himself. When equipment broke down or chores ran late, it was Andrew who took the tongue-lashings or cuffings. When Andrew and his brothers needed to head into town for parts or supplies—a reprieve from sun and soil—Andrew's father saw fit to go instead to vaunt his position to the townsfolk and often coming back home late and drunk.

Andrew detested his life on the farm. When he came of age, without forethought, he informed the family of his intentions to join a merchant vessel crew out of the Port of Norfolk. Andrew's father refused to drive him to the dockyards. Instead, Andrew shared goodbyes with his mother and brothers before walking seven hours into the city, with two green dollars and a biscuit in his pocket. He signed on with Old Dominion Steamship Company and never looked back. When he switched a year later to *Dismal Queen,* of the Atlantic Transport Line, he met Vincent and had since sailed with him and the present crew.

"It does look awfully a bit like Paris," said Andrew.

"You think the girls are just as dandy?" Vincent asked.

"They're not," came a gruff voice further along the taffrail. The pair turned to look at an approaching sailor, a middle-aged man with thick chin stubble and a perpetually surly countenance.

"What's that, Barry?" shouted Vincent over ship bells and

clamoring watercraft around them.

"I said, don't get your hopes up with these girls here. The Parisians are much more … accommodating than *porteñas*." He spoke with the comical lilt of a coherent drunkard.

"What are you saying?" Vincent asked.

"*Porteñas. Por TEH nyahs,*" he enunciated for emphasis. "That's what they call the girls here in Buenos Aires."

"No, no. What do you mean they aren't as 'accommodating'?"

"What I mean is, you'll have no luck with an Argentine girl: they ain't nothin' but papist wops to the core, and sin like the Virgin Mary—they ain't no Frenchies."

"They're Italian?" asked Vincent, raising an eyebrow. "This is South America. We were just in Santos only a few days ago. There's no Italians there."

"Yeah? Well, these here ain't no Brazilians, either now, isn't they? It's two different worlds from here and there. You need to know Spanish for these ones, and they actually want to chew the rag and not get to the business, see. You'll need to head on over to *El Nacional* if you want to wet your whistle. That's where the men'll be headin', if you two ain't fairies."

"What's El Nacional?" asked Vincent.

"It's a brothel, son, a *prostíbulo*, as they say. A place where you can get loaded on hooch and women, and they have the finest selection, you hear? Polaks, Russkis, gypsies, herms; it's a buffet of international pleasures."

A boyish grin grew across Vincent's face as he looked at Andrew.

"Say, you hear that?" he said excitedly. "Let's go! I'm overdo and itchin' for the company."

"I don't think so, Vince," said Andrew, tapping his fist on the railing. "I—I don't want to catch nothin'. And besides, we said it looks like Paris. I reckon we should verify if so."

Vincent rolled his eyes. "Don't be a pantywaist. We are *men*," he said, thumping his chest. "Let's do what men do best. And besides, you love a loose girl. Don't think I forgot about that sweet-eyed Dutch one you had in De Wallen." Andrew blushed. "See!" exclaimed Vincent. "Also, we've seen the *real* Paris, mind you. This is no Paris, which means it probably isn't worth a damn. You don't see Mr. Eiffel's fancy new tower, now, do you? And you can't beat that."

"Still, we've never been here before and won't be here long, most likely."

"I don't care what big bugs built the White Tower of Dover or the Count of Monte Cristo Château. I need a drink, and I need a broad," Vincent said, tapping his two fingers.

"We can get those anywhere."

"Pshaw! Did you not hear Barry? They've got Polish girls! Have you *seen* a Polish girl? I've only heard stories."

Andrew shook his head and grumbled; it was useless to convince Vincent otherwise.

"You're saying the girls are fine?" Andrew asked.

"Knockouts," replied Vincent.

Andrew stood up from the railing and fixed his cap. "All right, I'm game."

Vincent put his arm around Andrew's shoulder and shook him. "Atta-boy!"

Dismal Queen's ship bell jangled. Andrew, Vincent, and Barry were three of the sixty-eight crew members aboard, who took the signal as a sign to gather around the officers on the main deck. The docking gang slid the ship along the wharf's edge until it came to a halt. The boatswain's whistle bleated at a piercing frequency and quieted the crew.

Captain O'Kelly, a long-bearded old Irishman and master of the vessel, stepped forth wearing the typical sailor's navy peacoat, his head topped by a sea-weathered fisherman's cap, and sporting a smoldering corncob pipe propped on his shiny bottom lip. He began by going over several orders of business regarding managing the cargo, crew expectations, prospects from the superintendents of the shipping company, and some of the local laws and ordinances of the port city.

He closed his oration by saying, "Once we've resupplied and have the hold filled and tallied, we'll be outward bound for New York, to deliver. I suspect it'll take no more t'an t'ree days to get underway but listen for sooner. T'at suggests your shore leave is conditional; you must report in daily to staff before noon. If ye bunk off, ye be docked a day's wages. The port will be to our rudder before we make colors. T'is means you will report to your stations before six bells of the morning watch. If ye not here, then we cast off wit'out ye. Have I made meself clear?"

"Aye, sir," said the crew in unison.

"Grand, that's just grand! Take your shore leave t'en. Dismissed!"

The crew whooped and hollered, and dashed for the gangplank.

"You two comin'?" barked Barry.

Vincent snatched Andrew by his coat's lapel and yanked him along. "We are!" he shouted back.

Andrew ripped his jacket from Vincent's clutches. "Aye, take it easy. I'm coming," he replied.

Andrew and Vincent followed Barry and a few other seasoned sailors down the ramp and onto the main street of the dock. They headed north, weaving past mongers, children, and carts queuing against the brick facades of warehouses shaped like those of English terraced houses. The local men of the dikes dressed in workday shirts and britches, and topped themselves with wide brimmed hats. They dominated the scene with hardly a woman in sight. That is, until the trio reached El Nacional. After heading down by the southernmost dike and west into narrow cobblestone streets, past mansions and churches, they found El Nacional standing before them. A sturdy stone building housing a bar, nothing extraordinary, save for the flock of flamboyant prostitutes around it. The garish ladies stood outside, fluttering their kerchiefs and stretching their necklines at the herds of men eyeballing them like livestock for purchase. Vincent bit the edge of the scrunched-up cap in his fist and slapped it against his knee. "Hot damn!" he exclaimed.

The men waltzed into the bar. The clientele consisted of a variety of male specimens of the human species: gentlemen, side-eyed sweaty husbands, the eccentric, tradesmen, artists, joiners, teenagers too young, politicians too old, and, of course, sailors and seafarers alike. Andrew, Vincent, Barry, and the others from *Dismal Queen* took a table next to some British sailors in the corner of the parlor. The Brits banged their fists on the table and whistled at the passing escorts perusing the patrons. A server came by and delivered a tray of beers to their table. The sailors snatched them up like beggars, hoisted the *birras*, and clacked them together before taking gulps. As Andrew wiped the froth from his mouth, he noticed a man dressed in a pressed black jacket across the parlor, berating one of the prostitutes. She had her eyes downcast, and he had his finger and forehead inches from her nose. He pinched her chin and pushed it upwards to force her eyes upon him, but she pulled away. The man tightened his lips and struck her, hard. She did not flinch nor stumble but welcomed the blow like a loyal whipped dog. His berating grew louder, and Andrew could make out a Slavic dialect. The man then pointed to the table of *Dismal Queen* sailors. The girl nodded and trudged towards it. She kept her gaze fixed on the floor. The sailors clapped and coaxed her with whistles and cheers. One of the British sailors snatched her by her bruised wrist, jerked her close to him, and placed his hand under her bottom.

"She's still warm, lads!" he bellowed with a cheeky grin. The other sailors laughed and jibed at her.

Andrew studied her: she swayed on weak knees like a mast caught in a light pitch and wore an overdrawn skirt with pantalettes down to her garters. There was rouge lacquered across her cheeks and lips; her eyes bore thick black eyeliner, the lids smothered in a hazy sky-blue shade. Andrew realized the gaudy varnish and skirt were a means to cover the sallow, sunken, leaden skin and frail, beaten, used figure beneath. The girl turned her eyes upward and captured his gaze. Pale-azure eyes of forceful radiance stared back at him. They sparkled alone, isolated against a complexion drained of lushness and life. Looking at her brewed a sickening feeling in the pit of Andrew's stomach.

"I'm going to go," he announced quietly to Vincent. But as he stood up, Vincent seized him by the coattail.

"Wait, hold on. Where are you going? We—we just got here!"

"I don't feel like staying."

"Why not?"

"I just don't."

"Andy, come on. Don't do this."

"I'm going,"

"What are you—"

"Let him go!" Barry shouted, shoving Andrew away from the

table. Andrew turned and glared at Barry with fists clenched. "Don't spoil it for the rest of us. Take your cockamamie ass outta here or sit down and shut up. You'll have your turn."

Andrew kept his eyes on Barry, then glanced at Vincent, hoping he would follow. The other sailors shot sneers at Andrew. Vincent turned his nose and sipped his beer. Andrew took a long look at him and then nodded. He rolled his shoulders to set his coat, then made for the door.

Chapter 3

He stepped out into the intersection of the cobblestone streets. The sun shone thinly as a chilly spring breeze swept past the ankles of passersby. Andrew itched to stretch his legs and see what lay ahead in this new city. *Where to go?* he asked himself. Andrew looked above the rooftops and wagered that a grand steeple or lofty tower would lead him to a decent starting point. Nothing captured his liking. He needed a better line of sight and decided the wide cluster of train tracks between Puerto Madero and the bulk of the city would give him a better view. He set off down the street towards the port.

From this angle of view, Andrew could make out a portion of *Dismal Queen's* iron between the terraced warehouses from across the train tracks. As he crossed them, he retraced his thoughts back to the grand palace-like structure they had passed just as the ship entered the harbor and redirected his steps northward along the backside of the warehouses. A faded-pink palace appeared about half a mile ahead. Although there was much more open space on the city side of the warehouses, Andrew found himself squeezing to slip past an endless stream of horse-drawn wagons and carts loading and unloading their freight. The warehouse elevators lowered the cargo into the wains. Then, the driver would snap the reins, signaling the next wagon to take its place. The loaders chirped and chided one another; those currently idle chatted while passing among them hollowed gourds filled with infused herbs. A herd of bleary-eyed foreigners walked alongside Andrew, apparently fresh off an ocean liner. They babbled in Italian, mainly, mixed with hints of Spanish, French, Russian, and German. In an empty lot next to the train tracks, some schoolboys chased and kicked a leather *fútbol.* The ball skipped and hopped over the debris and tread-beaten soil. Pairs of scrap wood pieces shoved into the ground on each end of their play area acted as goalposts. Andrew recalled seeing the game played on the beaches of São Paulo and figured there must be a rising interest in it.

The fetid odors of steam engines, grease, and seawater reminded him of the coal piers in Norfolk. The memory made him feel more pleasant, as did moving among the *porteños.* Having spent weeks in tight metal cabins surrounded by sea-sky horizons and armpit-stained animals, seeing the exchanges of land-dwelling inhabitants was something he relished—the *porteños* in particular. They were an animated sort, speaking with cheery vigor and a fleeting regard for personal space when conversation intensified. Their hands bounced, swept, spun, pursed, and pointed; verbal expression was no more than a supporting act to their ardently performative limbs, in true *italiano* fashion. This charmed Andrew to the point of dismay, for his elementary knowledge of Spanish would not suffice for effective communication.

The palace sat atop a vast staircase that climbed gradually from the port waters. Andrew went up the steps and proceeded around the side of the eclectic structure, finding himself standing before a resplendent plaza. The crowd around him transformed from dockworkers and shoeless boys to men in three-piece suits and ladies with leg-o'-mutton-sleeves. The sound of clopping horse hooves and rolling carriage wheels echoed from the buildings and brick streets that surrounded the plaza. Hackney coaches collected and discarded aristocrats and dignitaries while people on foot scrambled to the sides of the streets to avoid being trampled. Andrew knew this was the place to start his big-city adventure. He noticed a few *Dismal Queen* crew mates enter the national *banco* a few meters from the palace, looking to exchange their fresh dollars for Argentine pesos. Andrew, who had collected quite a sum from several consecutive seafaring ventures, did likewise. His pockets jangled with fresh coins as he departed the bank, then snagged the first trolley just outside.

The horse-drawn conveyance followed the iron tracks in front of the Government House, known as *La Casa de Gobierno* or, to the locals, *La Casa Rosada* (the Pink House) for its baby-pink stone. Stylized with mansard roofs and Italian loggias, it crowned the end of the city square, known as the *Plaza de Mayo*. Rivaling it in elegance across the square was the elder white Spanish colonial building and former government house known as the *Cabildo*. A few steps north was the *Catedral Metropolitana,* or Metropolitan Cathedral. Built in the Greco-Roman revival style, it had a line of pillars at its front and a broad, triangular roof capped with a dome aft. The plaza's center was decorated with a flourish of lampposts, manicured trees and bushes, and a singular obelisk celebrating the country's successful revolution against its former monarchial Spanish rulers. Plaza de Mayo encapsulated Argentina's triumph, glory, and history with a splendor comparable to the grandest in Europe.

The trolley moved out of the square and up *Avenida de Mayo,* which ran through the heart of the city. On each side loomed the ubiquitous Parisian-style architecture he had admired earlier, with verdant trees that harked back to Paris's Champs-Élysées. Andrew had to crank his neck back and stretch his head out of the trolley window to fully appreciate the scale and sophistication of the buildings. Although confident the trolley would take him back to Puerto Madero, he felt the city far too marvelous to witness from a sitting position. He hopped off and took to the streets on foot. Pausing at the occasional street vendor to snag a pack of smokes or a handful of caramelized peanuts called *garrapiñadas,* he watched performers and buskers play out their skits and serenade with song—a far cry from his experience in El Nacional.

Andrew strolled onward until he was good and lost. The sun had hardly moved an inch in the afternoon sky, and *Dismal Queen* was not going anywhere. Following hours of chasing places where crowds gathered or monoliths beckoned, he stopped at one of the parks south of Avenida de Mayo to sit on a bench and rest his legs. Andrew popped a cigarette in his mouth and lit the end with a match while watching four men at a nearby table playing a card game called *truco.* As far as he could make out, it was a test of deception as much as of chance and riotously entertaining. Andrew grinned when one of the men teased the other for his poor attempt at furtively signaling to his partner. People picnicked and promenaded past the lakes and manicured trees. Andrew watched them go to and fro as he dragged from his cigarette. He had not intended to stay long, but the pleasant scene was lulling. His eyelids began to dip, so he flicked the butt, tilted his sailor cap down, and settled in for a decidedly short nap.

"*Señor, no puede dormir acá,*" came a voice. It was a policeman walking the beat, nudging Andrew's shoulder. Andrew lay on his side with his hands tucked beneath his armpits. He opened his eyes to a fading orange sky and speckled purplish clouds.

"Ah, hell," he grumbled.

"*¿Disculpe?*" asked the policeman, one eyebrow rising in curiosity.

"Sorry, um, *low see-en-toe, grah-see-yahs,*" Andrew apologized in his limited Spanish.

The officer gave him an eye and carried on. Andrew stepped lively out of the empty park and hurried toward what he thought was Avenida de Mayo. But nothing seemed familiar. The sunset was at his back, meaning Puerto Madero was somewhere ahead of him. He decided to head that way, favoring roads turning right. He would inevitably run into either the port or El Nacional, he thought, and carried on with his hands in his pockets. When the stars were in full bloom, he recognized the steeple of a church he had passed on his way to El Nacional. He was sure he knew where to go from here and slowed his pace. He progressed down an empty street with shoddy lighting and hummed a tune to the rhythm of his footsteps. Then, a sudden blood-curdling shriek split the air.

Chapter 4

Andrew cautiously approached the corner whence came the shriek, hearing other voices. He thought to ignore the situation, knowing what complications could come from foreign sailors meddling in local issues. But when there was another scream, curiosity overcame his caution. He sped to the corner and peered around it, spotting a man grappling with two women: one clawed and kicked, attempting to break free from the man's clutches; the other yanked and held his arm and leg.

"Puść mnie, ty mała zdziro!" bellowed the man in Polish at the woman yanking his arm.

"¡Dejala ir, mal parido!" she cursed back, imploring the man to free the other woman.

He wrenched his arm back and forth, trying to loosen it from one woman's grip while grasping the other woman, still fighting against him. She blubbered and screamed, and the opposing forces split and tore the seams of her skirt. Andrew gave in to impulse.

"Hey!" he shouted. The struggling three did not hear him. "Hey! Stop!"

The Polish man turned to see Andrew approaching. *"Co do diabła? Amerykanin?"* he muttered, apparently viewing

Andrew's accent and imposition as both an irregularity and threat.

The situation had Andrew slightly bewildered, too. *"Señor, por favor,"* Andrew pleaded with palms raised.

"Wynocha, Amerykanin; to nie twoja sprawa," the man barked at him.

He didn't need to understand the words to know this was a warning. "Sir," he continued, "Let the woman go now. Let. Go."

The man growled. He tossed the blubbering woman onto the cobblestones. The other woman went to reach for her, but the man stepped over her and pinched her between his ankles. He reached into his pocket and drew from it a slender piece. The device clicked, and Andrew's eyes darted down to the glint of a switchblade. The man swiped at the woman who was reaching for his prey. Andrew lunged for the man and took him to the ground with a bear hug. Andrew held the man to his back, their chests pinning between them the knife-wielding hand. The man wedged his other hand in between them, pulled the blade free, and reared it back. Andrew, who had his arms stuck beneath the man, rolled to his side to free his left arm. As the blade sped toward his face, he threw his arm over his eyes.

A sharp pain shot through Andrew's arm as the blade pierced through the tender underside of his forearm and sank to the grip. He let out a forceful grunt as the man twisted it—scrapping the bone. A geyser of blood trailed as the man unplugged the knife. Andrew felt the man's muscles tense, readying to deliver another blow. Gripped with anger and adrenaline, Andrew caught the man's wrist inches from his face and managed to situate his feet beneath himself. He shoved his knee into the man's gut, and air flushed from his lungs. A gurgled wheezing sound followed, and the man keeled over onto his back. With both arms free, Andrew proceeded to careen his fist repetitively into the man's jaw. His knuckles chafed as he abused the man's face again, and again, and again.

"You stupid bastard!" Andrew said as he served each word with some spittle and a fist. He struck the man several more times before standing up and sending his boot to the side of the man's skull. The head lurched upward, then fell to the street with a hollow thud. Blood dribbled from the corner of his mouth as the man lay unconscious. Andrew surveyed the damage he had done before touching his arm. He could not see it well since the light from the lamppost was dim, but he felt a warm ooze spilling down his sleeve from the gash and dripping from his fingers. The two women looked at him with wide eyes.

"You two all right?" Andrew gasped.

They did not move nor speak. Andrew took a step forward, but dizziness overcame him. He stumbled, and the women sprang to his side, grabbing him by each arm.

"I'm fine, I'm fine," Andrew said, attempting to straighten up.

"*Tenemos que ayudarlo,*" said the tear-stained woman, her Spanish inflected with a Polish accent, insisting on helping him.

"*Ya tuvimos suficientes problemas y ¿ahora tengo que salvar a un yanqui?*" countered the other. Her Spanish sounded local and natural.

"*Él viene con nosotros,*" insisted the Pole.

"*Nos va a atrasar,*" said the Argentine.

"*¡Él viene!*"

"Whatever you ladies are planning to do," Andrew interjected faintly, "Do it quickly. I'm starting to—I'm starting to feel a little dizzy."

The two women looked at each other until the Argentine conceded with a "*¡Bien!*"

They guided Andrew through empty streets and back alleyways for nearly a mile before reaching a set of apartment-like homes stacked against a hill, like a slipshod set of dominoes with labyrinths of staircases leading into dark cavities.

They went past one of the staircases and into a bend where a door had been wedged into a nook between two apartments. The Argentine woman turned to look at him. Andrew, covered in blood and sweat, struggled to keep his eyes open. The Polish woman remained silent but kept her grip tight around him. The Argentine rapped on the door, and the muffled sound of shuffling feet came from behind it.

"*¿Quién es?*" came a voice from the other side.

"*Ezra, soy yo, Renata con Danuta! ¡Abrí!*" the *porteña* said in a low voice.

The door opened, and a man poked his head out. He was evidently Polish, with a shaved bony face, rounded widow's peak, circular glasses, and a narrow mouth.

"*Pasa,*" he whispered, gesturing them inside. Renata entered the abode, followed by Andrew and the Polish woman named Danuta.

"*¿Quién es? Dios mío, ¡¿qué pasó?!*" demanded Ezra, noticing the state of the blood-stained man and disheveled women. Renata began to tell the tale of her rescue of Danuta from the brothel, after which she had been attacked by one of the owners, the *rufianes*. Ezra questioned every one of the details: What did he look like? Why did you say it like that? Did he recognize you? Were you followed? Renata answered each query with diminishing patience. He then proceeded to lecture her about the dangers of the *rufianes* discovering their operation and blamed her for the botched rescue. Danuta snapped at Ezra in Polish, insisting Renata was not to blame, and begged Ezra to help her rescuer.

Beads of sweat formed like condensation across Andrew's pallid face. Danuta held him, braced against a pillar. Ezra approached and rolled up Andrew's bloodied sleeve, revealing the puncture in the flesh, from which blood continued to dribble out. The look on Ezra's face indicated that his situation was dire. Danuta pleaded again for Ezra's help, but the wispy Pole refused and insisted that Andrew's mere presence had already compromised their lives and his operation. Danuta volleyed a rage-filled whirl of contempt at Ezra and threatened to leave if he refused further. Ezra, dismissing the threat, told her to go, if she wished to fall victim to the *rufianes*. Renata—who apparently did not understand Polish—demanded an explanation for all the bickering, which Ezra clarified. Seeing that neither Danuta nor Ezra would concede, Renata announced that she would take Andrew to her parents' home. Ezra, who only wanted to free himself of this situation, did not question it and insisted Danuta should say her goodbyes. The three of them helped Andrew to the door, and Danuta wrapped her frail arms around Renata.

"*Gracias por todo,*" she said, thanking her.

"*De nada. Que encuentres tu paz, querida niña,*" replied Renata, wishing her peace while they exchanged the *beso en la mejilla*, the traditional Argentine cheek kiss. Danuta turned her gaze to Andrew. His eyes sagged, and his head bounced and swayed on a weak neck. She raised herself up on her toes, placed her hands on his temples, and planted a kiss on his forehead.

"*Dziękuje bardzo. Muchas gracias, señor,*" she said softly to him.

Andrew's eyes peeked open enough to notice Danuta's vibrant

pale-azure eyes under awnings of smeared blue eyeshadow.

"Hey," he mumbled. "I know you."

Danuta nodded as she brushed his cheek, tears welling in her eyes. Ezra placed his hands on her shoulders and held her back. Turning to Renata, he urged her to go. She nodded and placed Andrew's arm over her shoulder, and stepped into the street.

Chapter 5

"Dale, mové las piernas," Renata grumbled, praying his rubber legs would discover their purpose. She had to find immense strength to lug the sailor's deadening weight of a hundred and eighty pounds; she was nearly a foot shorter and seventy pounds lighter.

"I don't know what you are saying," he groaned, "But I hope that means we are close, because I can't feel my feet."

Murmurs came from loitering shapes behind the orange smolder of cigarettes, looking on as Renata navigated through the streets. One of them stepped toward her.

"Che, muchacha, ¿necesitás ayuda?" he said, offering his services.

"No, gracias," she replied. She steered herself and Andrew away from him. *"Es mi hermano. Está un poco en pedo. No pasa nada."*

Renata's lie sold, for the man kept his distance. They reached a two-story tenement house, on a shabby street where a shallow gutter ran through the middle. Each block appeared to be an amalgam of apartments. The similar doors and sparse windows made it nearly impossible to discern where a dwelling began and ended. Renata steadied Andrew against the side of one of the homes, then knocked on its door.

"¡Es mejor que sea su fantasma llamando a mi puerta, o la voy a mandar a la tumba yo misma!" grumbled a woman on the other side. Her voice grew louder as she neared the door. Just as it opened, Andrew's eyes rolled into the back of his head. His legs gave way, and he fell headlong through its threshold, pulling down Renata, who let out a yelp. The woman who answered the door shrieked as the full weight of Andrew's mass slammed Renata to the floor. She groaned as she lay buried beneath the sailor, but the wailing of the woman at the door brought her to her feet.

"¡Mamá, Mamá!" Renata rasped. She held her side as she attempted to placate the panicking woman. Renata's mother, of similar frame and stature to her daughter, was dressed in a nightgown. She clutched her chest and continued to belt out in horror.

"Mamá, tranquila. ¡Soy yo!" pleaded Renata, hoping to salve her mother's hysterics.

The home was pitch dark but for the shaky candle in Mamá's hand. At last, she forced a peek at her daughter and Andrew—whose blood now covered both of them. She bellowed louder.

"¡Ay, Dios mío! ¡Dios mío, hija! ¡Dios mío, toma mi alma!" Mamá cried to God. She repeatedly made the sign of the cross. *"Renata, ¡¿qué estás haciendo con un hombre muerto?!"* she demanded, assuming Andrew was dead. Her eyes bulged from their sockets as she gazed upon his seemingly lifeless body. Renata assured her mother that he was not dead but had only fainted.

A voice from down the hall barked, asking what the commotion was. Emerging from the shadows came Papá, Renata's father, in a half-buttoned union suit and brandishing a revolver. He was a square-shaped man with a receding hairline and a thick, dark mustache. The top of his head was barren of follicular growth, but his chest brimmed with it. His eyes turned to his wife, then to his daughter, and then to Andrew. He glared at Renata and demanded an explanation. As she seemed unable to find the words, Papá assumed the worst. He cocked the hammer of the revolver and pointed its barrel at the back of Andrew's head.

"*¡No, Papá, no!*" shouted Renata.

"*¡Necesito agua! ¡Necesito agua!*" cried Mamá, clutching her chest.

Renata managed to string together words that told Papá of Andrew's bravery in facing the attacker. He peered into Renata's eyes to confirm that this tale was true before easing the hammer back against the primer. He bent down to roll the sailor over and noted his shallow breathing and milky-gray face.

"*Se ve terrible,*" Papá said with bland shock. Renata rolled her eyes. He then directed his daughter to bring some wet rags for the sailor and water for her mother. She pried the candlestick from Mamá and hurried to the back of the home to the kitchen.

Renata returned momentarily and tilted the water cup up to her mother's lips. "*Tomá, Mamá. Tomá,*" Renata whispered. Papá grabbed Andrew under the arms and dragged him to a straw mattress in an adjacent room and laid him upon it. Renata took another cup, filled it with water, and gently poured it down Andrew's gullet. She steadied his head to ensure it took. Papá ordered his quivering wife to come and help. Throughout the night, Mamá and Renata tended to Andrew, taking shifts to ensure he remained stable and that his breathing did not fall shallow.

Chapter 6

A chilling drop of liquid slid from Andrew's forehead and down the side of his nose. It tickled his face. The moment his eyelids peeled apart, a blaring white light blinded his sight. Andrew shut his eyes tight, then tried to open them again. But the light rendered his vision useless. He felt a wave of panic as he began to recall the events of last night. He remembered little, but enough to recall the attacker, the two women, the fight, the wound, and his fading consciousness.

I'm dead; that man did me in, Andrew thought. His body felt numb; the sensations of his limbs felt foreign and static. He thought he had passed. As he processed this fate, a darkness swept over him, and the persistent glare ceased. He shuddered at the thought of what force from the afterlife had come to collect him. He braved his eyes open. An ecliptic ring glimmered around a silhouette before him, nothing more than a smudge in his impaired sight. His pupils flexed and tightened until the facial outline was revealed to be that of a woman, a woman with a gentle complexion, skin like ivory, delicate waves of deep brown hair draping over him like vines of a weeping willow, and mindful hazel eyes set upon him. He fell into their depths as a liquefied, cooling sensation trickled over his forehead.

"Are you an angel?" he muttered.

The woman reared her head back. *"¿Hablaste?"* she asked. Her voice was echoic and distant, but somehow familiar.

"Am I dead?" he asked.

The woman turned her head away. *"¡Mamá!"* she shouted, *"¡Él habló!"*

"Dying. That wasn't so bad," Andrew added.

A woman appeared next to the angel and peered down at him. *"¿Qué dijo?"* she asked her daughter what Andrew had said.

"No sé; no hablo ingles," replied the angel, shrugging.

Hearing the angel speak Spanish triggered a realignment of his entropic sensibilities to a singular point of mortal self-awareness. In a confused panic, Andrew launched himself upwards with a jolt.

"¡Che, che, che!" chirped Mamá. She knelt beside the angel and grabbed his shoulder and chest. *"Renata, ayúdame a acostarlo,"* she commanded her daughter. The angel threw her hands on the sailor. The two restrained him from rising any further. *"Calmate, muchacho. Calmate."*

Andrew's eyes darted around the shabby room. The calm collected nature of the women eased him, and the sudden rise had made him dizzy. The two women eased his head back on the pillow. The cooling sensation returned, and he noted that it was the drip of a damp rag and the angel who held it was but a mortal woman. The golden streamers that had lined her edges were no halo but daybreak through a window. He felt grounded and thankful.

"Oh, thank you, God. Thank you, God," he breathed.

Renata continued to dab and wet the cloth over his sweltering forehead. At the same time, Mamá lifted a wooden ladle to his lips.

"Sopa, sopa. Tome de a sorbos," Mamá insisted. Lentils, onions, beef, and pork slid down Andrew's throat. He lipped the spoon; never had a stew tasted so rich to him as at that moment. He relished the flavor and warmth. Mamá filled the spoon again, and Andrew's maw clenched around the back of its bowl. She held it up to her eye, commenting on the indentations of the fresh bite marks. Renata uttered her sympathies, but Mamá ensured her the blame for Andrew's plight was entirely her daughter's. She began with recriminations of Renata's brazen disregard for curfew. Renata groaned and rolled her eyes at the return of a familiar lecture. Hoping her overt exasperation would disarm her mother, Renata insisted she lost her way following a fruitless late-evening venture for flour. Mamá scoffed with a deep chuckle and pursued her interrogation with a barrage of inquiries as to the events and her whereabouts last night. She waved the soup spoon about like the gavel of an accusatory magistrate, flinging its residue. Throughout the increasing vitriol, Renata maintained her innocence. Mamá moved for an anecdotal approach, citing a neighbor's report of seeing Renata leaving a *prostíbulo* no more than a fortnight ago. This made Renata's cheeks flush. Puddles formed in Mamá's eyes. Renata dismissed this as gossip and continued to focus on tending to Andrew, for guilt would not let her look at her mother.

"¡Cálmensen!" boomed a voice from outside the room. The women turned to look at the doorway where Papá stood. Mamá lowered her cocked backhand aimed at her daughter. Before Mamá could detail the findings from her cross-examination to her spouse, Papá grunted and threw his hand over his shoulder to signal he would not hear it.

He lumbered into the room and approached Andrew. He

stood over the sailor with his meaty hands on his hips and asked his wife and daughter for an update on Andrew's health. Renata jumped to reply and reported that he had awakened recently and would likely make a full recovery. Andrew lay bare-chested and supine, with his bandaged arm across his torso. He groaned as he let out exhalations. His eyes flickered between resting and awake. Renata added that Andrew would need a new shirt. Papá, agreeable to the notion, asked his daughter to retrieve one of his shirts from his bedroom.

As Renata left the room, Mamá shot to her feet and squared off with her husband, directing her energies to him now. She declared they had reared a deceitful daughter to the extent that her antics had blackened the family's good name. Papá dismissed these claims as female dramatics. Invective followed, concluding that Papá was no more than a denier and a fool of the highest order. She insisted he must find their daughter a suitable husband, to steady her. Again, Papá scoffed, claiming no man in the *barrio* was worthy of his daughter's hand. If that was true, Mamá opined, then they must send her away to live with Papá's sister in the countryside—deep in the southern interior of Argentina. There, she was certain Renata would learn docility, and it would keep her away from immoral influences. Just as Mamá said this, Renata entered the room with a patched shirt. She kept her head down, as if their shouts did not carry into every room of the modest home. She set the shirt on a stool next to Andrew.

"Up, up," she said.

Andrew, his mouth open like a fish, nodded. He took a moment to brace himself. As he pressed his elbows into the mattress, searing pain shot through his arm. He winced and tucked it in. Renata reached for him. He readjusted his weight onto his other elbow and proceeded to hoist himself upright. Renata guided him, then shoved a few pillows and blankets into the small of his back for support.

"Thank you. I mean, *grah-see-ahs*," Andrew said.

"*De nada*," replied Papá, leaning over with a deliberate head nod. He motioned to the shirt on the stool. Renata held it up.

"Oh," exclaimed Andrew. "Why, thank you. *Moo-choh grah-see-ahs*."

Papá grunted in approval. Andrew rose to his feet. The room spun, and his knees had the consistency of rubber. He fell forward. All three grabbed him before gravity had a chance to send him to the floor. They steadied him as Renata inserted Andrew's arms into the sleeves of the *remera*. She stood before him to button it together. Andrew watched as she cinched each one. She peered upwards at him through the tops of her eyes, stirring a tingling sensation down the sides of his neck. Her cheeks reddened. She darted her eyes back to the shirt. After she fed the last button through, she tautened the hem and brushed the shoulders.

Mamá prompted with a cough before asking when Papá would take the man back to Puerto Madero. The father looked between Andrew and his daughter before declaring that he would not take him and that he would leave this task to Renata. Mamá's jaw fell to the floor. Papá left to put his work clothes on, and her tirade followed after him. Renata set Andrew's brogans before him.

"*¡Dale!*" Renata whispered excitedly.

"Huh?" responded Andrew.

"*¡Dale!* Shoes. Put shoes!"

Andrew shoved his feet into the boots and Renata laced them. She grabbed him by the hand and led him out the front door.

Chapter 7

"My coat. I need my coat," he said to her.

"*¿Qué?*" she asked.

"I need my coat. It's a little chilly," he replied. Andrew simulated the act of gripping the lapels of his peacoat.

"*Ah, tu campara,*" she exclaimed. "*¿Por qué creés que hablar más lento va a ayudar?*"

"Yes, I need it?" he continued. "*Dohn-day es-tah mi* coat?"

"No ready. No ready," she replied.

"No ready?"

"*Sí.* Ch-yes."

She then pointed to her arm near the same area where Andrew had his knife wound. "*Agujero,*" she added.

"*Agoo*-huh?" he said, squinting his eyes.

Renata rolled her eyes and mimicked the action of a knife going through her arm and then sewing with needle and thread. "*Agujero,*" she repeated.

"Oh!" Andrew slapped his palm on his forehead. "It is not ready because there is a hole in it. You want to fix it first. Gotcha."

Renata nodded; they had an accord. They set off through the streets of La Boca. Andrew had no recollection of passing through it last night. Men trekked through the neighborhood with lunch tins and knapsacks in hand and over shoulders. The women had their wash buckets and children out, ready for a cleaning. Hawkers toiled and poor men ambled, asking for spare coins. Andrew and Renata weaved through the throng. The bustle never ceased even after they left La Boca. When they reached the docks of Puerto Madero, Andrew let out a sigh of relief. *Dismal Queen* sat moored and familiar to him. A crane lowered a pallet of cereals into its hold. Men on board steadied the cargo as the jib dipped and swiveled. An overwhelming feeling of gratitude compelled Andrew to wrap his good arm around Renata. His chest pressed into her nose, and she reared her head back with an awkward grin.

"*Bueno, bueno, yanqui,*" grunted Renata. Andrew let her go and looked at her with a smile.

"*¡Gra-see-ahs!* I cannot thank you and your parents enough."

"*De nada,*" she responded. "*Muchas gracias por ayudarme anoche. De todo corazón.*"

Andrew nodded. "*Day nada.* I don't even know who you are, but I will never forget you or this night. By the way, what is your name? Um, *¿co-moe tay yamas?*" he asked, extending his hand out for a handshake.

Renata giggled. "*Me llamo Renata,*" she replied.

"*Rey-naw-duh.*"

"*Sí, ¿y vos? ¿Cómo te llamas?*"

"Andrew," he said, pointing to himself. "My name is Andrew."

"Ann-jeh-roo," she repeated slowly.

He nodded. "*¡Sí!* That'll do."

She gave him a beaming smile. "*¡Mira!*" she said. Her tone changed to something more serious. She pointed at an imaginary watch on her wrist, then showed all of her fingers on one hand. "*Antes de las cinco, te voy a traer tu campera.*" She finished by gripping the lapels of the invisible coat as Andrew did earlier.

"Five o'clock, *cinco* o'clock, you will bring my coat?" he reaffirmed.

She nodded. "*Sí.*"

"Here?" he added, pointing downward.

"*Sí, acá. A este lugar.*" She pointed the same.

"Perfect, I will see you then," he said, pointing at his eyes and then at her. Having managed to communicate this, they both gave a smile.

"*¡Chau!*" she said with a wave.

"*¡Chow!*" Andrew replied, giving a casual salute. He felt silly for doing so.

As she turned around, an unsuspecting sailor barreled into her. It was Vincent. Renata stumbled back, but Vincent caught her by the arm just before she hit the ground.

"Easy there, sweetheart. You're going to hurt yourself," he said with a silver grin. Renata looked at him and sneered.

"Fine. Go on, shoo fly," he said, pushing her off.

Renata muttered something under her breath and carried on. Vincent took a blatant gander at her backside before turning toward Andrew. He noticed he still had eyes on Renata.

"Were you with that?" Vincent asked with raised brows.

Andrew looked at him and said nothing. Vincent gave him a playful jab.

"You were, weren't you?!" Andrew shook his head and started for *Dismal Queen.* "You sly bastard! With a *porteña* no less!"

"Shut it," said Andrew.

"Aye!" shouted Vincent to some of the nearby sailors, "Get a load of this guy; got his wick oiled by a *porteña!*"

A company of approaching sailors gave congratulatory

snickers—Vincent along with them. With his good arm, Andrew grabbed Vincent by the front of his shirt.

"I said, that's enough. Nothing happened, and now you're starting to eat at me."

"Hey, take it easy, tough guy," Vincent said. Andrew's knuckles dug into his chest. "It was just a tickle. You had better luck than some of us, anyway."

"I said nothing happened with the girl!"

"All right, all right, I believe you." Vincent tossed his hands up. "But get this. After you lit out from El Nacional, we had a few of the girls passed around, right, and before you know it, the owner bounced us and then—get this—*banned* us from the place!"

"Banned? What for?"

"No one knows! Apparently, someone got into a scrap with the owner's brother, or cousin, or something like that. A bunch of serious polak fellas, they were. Brought the guy in to see if he could tell if it was one of us. I tell you," Vincent chuckled, "his face looked like it was run through a gristmill and kicked by a mule. I reckon he couldn't see the fingers on his hands, he was so swollen up."

"Really? Do they know who did it?" Andrew's voice jumped an octave, and he slid his right hand into his pocket.

"No. None of us."

"It wasn't just that," came a grumpy voice.

It was Barry, with a couple of the other sailors in tow. His eyes were bloodshot.

"What was it, then? I could hardly understand the kike bastards," asked Vincent.

"Quiet, you!" snarled Barry. "Do you want one of them to hear you?" Vincent reared his head back and raised his eyebrows.

"Those 'bastards' are not to be trifled with, you hear? They're serious gangsters, real serious. They've got dough in deep pockets, and their hands run plum-deep through this city. They can do you in and make nobody think nothing of it. I was certain one of them was going to kill us back at ol' Nacional."

"They had me nervous. Why didn't we just go to another brothel, though?" asked Vincent.

"Like I say, they are some serious fellas; they own half the town's *prostíbulos*. We are banned from most anywhere that has some decent tail."

"Jesus, I didn't know all that. What were they sore at us for, then?"

"From what I gathered from one of them, some local bitch has been thieving their girls and got caught last night, but then some galoot stepped in and helped her and the hooker escape; they say it's one of us. He tore him up good—the beat one. You saw how he looked."

"Yeah." Vincent laughed again. "I was just telling ol' Andrew here about him."

"Yeah?" said Barry, looking over Andrew with a curious expression. "Where were you last night, after you went yellow and bitched?"

"He had a grind with a *porteña*!" Vincent giggled.

"Hogwash. I don't believe it; nobody can have a *porteña*, especially this betty."

"He did! I saw her!"

"Is that a fact?" Barry asked, surveying Andrew. "What she look like?"

"I don't know, I only got a look at her stern," Vincent added.

Barry continued to dress down Andrew with his eyes. "Where is your coat?" he asked Andrew.

"My what?" replied Andrew. He pretended not to hear Barry so that he could craft an answer.

"Your coat. The same one we all got. Where is it?"

"Say, he's right," said Vincent. "Where is your coat?"

Andrew looked between them. "I—I left it," he replied.

"You left it? What do you mean you left it?" Barry said.

Andrew's lips tightened. "At the *porteña's* house."

Vincent slapped his knee. "Ha! You son of a bitch! You left it so you could go back for seconds, now, didn't you?" Andrew gave an awkward nod and a grin. For the first time, Andrew was thankful for Vincent's need to hear himself talk. He waited for a response from Barry, who still glared at him with arms crossed. "You really are a sly bastard!" Vincent said, pointing a cockeyed thumb at Andrew. "This kid is pulling tricks from books I never did read."

Barry twisted his lips and eased his shoulders back. "I may have to see this girl myself, now we got nowheres to go," he said. "I've been at least fifteen years longer than you before the mast. I should have her myself before you again."

Andrew's ears went hot. "Hardly a qualification, wouldn't you say?" The words leaped from Andrew's lips.

"How's it you get her in one night, then? *Porteñas* have never been the sort, and you don't got it in you without a pocketbook."

"It just happened," said Andrew. "She took a liking, I suppose."

"I don't believe that for a second," Barry scoffed. "You give me my turn." He pointed at himself and stepped toward Andrew. The reek of ripened beer oozed from his chin. Andrew held his breath.

"Relax, you ol' masher," said Vincent. "Let him have his night with the broad. We set sail tomorrow anyway."

"We do?" asked Andrew, startled.

"Captain's orders. You better bring your coat before sunup this time," he said, giving Andrew a swat on the back.

"Where did you meet this girl? Is she a brothel's keep?" asked Barry.

"No," replied Andrew. "No, I met her in the city." He wished he had lied.

"Oh yeah? You look pretty spent for someone pulling rig for a living. She must've done a number on you last night."

"She sure did!" Vincent exclaimed. "Look at that face—he's whiter than milk fresh out the cow."

"I suppose," said Andrew. His placid stare took much of his willpower to maintain through Barry's interrogation. He feared any crooked grimace or grin would mean instant incrimination.

"You didn't see nothing last night about the Jews' hooker now, did you?" Barry asked.

"No," replied Andrew. "I don't know anything about that."

Barry eyed Andrew one more time, then sucked his teeth and fixed his cap. "Well, I hope not. Those Jews are looking for her. The salt that took part in this is in for a reckoning. If either of you find out anything, you come and tell me, you hear?" Andrew and Vincent nodded. Barry looked between the two before making for the ship.

Chapter 8

Andrew paced along *Dismal Queen's* railing. He prayed Renata would arrive soon and tried to keep his fevered glances at the spot where they parted subtle. The tangelo glow of the fading sun shimmered against the waters of Puerto Madero before he spotted her coming through the crowd. She wore a poppy red dress adorned with a shawl and carried Andrew's navy peacoat tucked under her arm. Andrew jogged down the gangplank. Renata stopped in her tracks when she saw him bearing down on her.

"*¿Qué pasa?*" she asked in a startled voice.

"We need to go," said Andrew. She loosened her grip around the coat and handed it to Andrew. He slung it over his shoulders and filled the sleeves in one swift motion.

"*¿Qué está pasando?*" Renata begged to know. Andrew grabbed her arm and led her away from the docks. "*¡Decime, qué pasa!*" The dock workers trudging home turned their heads at them.

"I'll explain later. Just trust me."

Renata gave Andrew a side-eye. He softened his gaze and held his hand out. Renata paused, then took it.

"Hey!" cried a voice from *Dismal Queen's* deck. Renata turned around to see who it was, but Andrew pulled her along without a glance. He led her past the warehouses and across the train tracks towards Chile Street. They pressed on until they arrived at the humming thoroughfare of Avenida Paseo Colón. Andrew looked around for a place to go. He noticed a recess in one of the buildings up ahead and ducked into its shadow. He peered out and looked around. Nobody was around to see them. Renata waited, studying Andrew. Andrew eased back into the alleyway and turned towards the confused *porteña*.

"*¿Qué está pasando?*" she demanded.

"They are looking for us," replied Andrew. Renata gave him a blank stare. Andrew sighed. "They," he said, pointing to at the knife wound, "are looking for us." He pointed at his eyes and then between himself and Renata.

"*Veo tu herida,*" she responded purposefully, pointing her cupped hands at his injured arm. "*¿Necesitás que revise tus vendajes?*" she asked, looking up at him.

"Yes," he replied with an assuring nod. "Them, the Polish—Jewish fella, or whoever he is a part of that attacked you—they, they are looking for us."

"*Dale,*" she insisted, "*Me dejas verla.*" She motioned for Andrew to take off his peacoat. Andrew looked at her funny.

"What do you need my coat for? Are you cold?" he asked.

She nodded and motioned again for the coat. Andrew removed the peacoat and slung it over her. She looked between her shoulders as the coat nestled over them. She raised an eyebrow.

"*¿Quién soy yo? ¿De la realeza?. ¿Por qué me ponés la campera?*" she asked in bewilderment. "*Arremangate y dejarme ver los vendajes.*" She rolled her fingers like she was folding a pie crust while focusing on his injured arm.

"I don't understand. Do you want to see my arm?"

Renata continued to motion for him to roll up his sleeve, and it started to annoy her. "*¡Dale!*"

"No, no *dah-lay*," Andrew said. "That's not what I meant. What I am saying is we are in danger." He flashed his palms like they were some type of warning light. Renata paused, pinched her fingers into a cone shape, and bobbed them, looking even more dumbfounded.

"*No entiendo lo que estás tratando de decir. ¿Qué querés?* Wuht shu wuhnt?" Renata asked.

Andrew knew his attempts to convey the danger they were in were useless. He again stretched his neck out from the alleyway and looked around. He noticed a bookshop about a quarter block down. Andrew took Renata by the hand and led her towards it. Just as they arrived, the bookkeeper was closing up.

"Excuse me! Umm, *pare-dohn-eh!*" shouted Andrew. The old bookkeeper pivoted slowly to see who it was.

"*¡Pare-dohn-eh, sen-yore!*" said Andrew.

"*¿Sí?*" replied the scruffy bookkeeper.

Andrew reverted to his gesticulation. "Can I … see … your books?" he said. He motioned each time between the pauses from himself, to his eyes, then to the books through the window. "I have money. *Tang-o dee-nare-o,*" he said, rubbing his thumb and the inside of his index finger together.

The bookkeeper waved him off. "*No, no,*" he said. "*Tengo una esposa e hijos que ver. Estoy cerrando la librería.*"

"*Por favor, señor,*" blurted out Renata, "*Nos concedería un momento. Vamos a ser rápidos.*"

Andrew turned to look at her and raised his eyebrows. The bookkeeper looked at her and softened. "*Pasen, pasen,*" he grumbled with a defeated sigh. "*Sean rápidos.*"

"*Gracias, señor,*" said Renata.

"*Sí, grah-see-uhs,*" said Andrew.

The bookkeeper stood with arms crossed and tapping his finger. Two kerosene lamps hovered over the musty stacks of books lining the walls. The stale smell of forgotten pages lingered. Each shelf bore labels referring to a particular genre of literature. Andrew stopped at one with the word *Diccionarios*. He filed through them until he came across a tawny pocket-sized dictionary titled *Diccionario: Inglés/Español – Español/Inglés*. He picked it up, flipped through the pages, then showed it to Renata.

"*¡Ahh, claro!*" she said with a nod. She turned to the bookkeeper. "*¿Cuánto cuesta?*" she asked.

"*Veinticinco centavos,*" said the bookkeeper.

Renata looked back at Andrew and held up two fingers, followed by five. Andrew reached into his pocket and withdrew some silver coins. He handed them to the man.

"*¡Grah-see-uhs!*" said Andrew.

"*De nada,*" replied the bookkeeper. He motioned for the door. "*Ahora sí por favor, ¿pueden salir de mi librería?*"

Andrew and Renata stepped outside under one of the Victorian lampposts that lined the wide streets of Avenida Paseo Colón. Andrew flicked through the dictionary and pointed to each word:

We—*Nosotros/Us*

Are—*Estar*

In—*En*

Danger—*Peligro*

Renata looked up at him and asked, "*¿Estamos en peligro?*"

He continued:

They—*Ellos*

Are—*Estar*

Search—*Buscar*

For—*Por*
Us—*Nos*
"*Ellos, ¿quiénes son 'ellos'?*" Andrew simulated a knife entering his arm. "*¿El hombre que te apuñaló?*" There was a hint of fright in her voice. He knew she understood and replied with a nod. Renata clutched her chest and turned away from Andrew for a moment. After a few pensive moments, she motioned for the dictionary, turned to the back of it, and pointed at the words as he had done:
Ellos—They
Saber—Know
Que—That/Than/What
Fuimos—We were
Nosotros—We/Us
"They know that we were us," Andrew said aloud in a confused tone. Renata shrugged. Andrew paused to decipher.

"Ahh! Do they know it was us?" he exclaimed. Renata shrugged more assuredly.

"I don't know," he said. He reached for the dictionary:
I—*Yo*
Do—*Hacer*
Not—*No*
Know—*Saber*
He pointed.
"*No lo sé,*" she said to him.
"*No low say,*" he repeated back to her.

She nodded and became pensive again. Andrew waited and watched her nibble on the edge of her fingers. She looked at him and grabbed him by the hand.

"*Dale,*" she commanded.

This time, she led the way, keeping them close to the buildings.

She moved with natural discretion, as if she had an innate understanding of spaces where eyes did not care to wander. They were heading southwest. Andrew started to recognize some of the roads and the unquestionable *conventillos,* the tenements of La Boca. They passed under some stairs and around the bend to the front door of Ezra's safe house. Renata knocked. They listened but heard nothing. She rapped the door again.

"*¿Quién es?*" came Ezra's voice from behind the door.

"*Ezra,*" whispered Renata, "*Soy yo, Renata.*"

The door opened enough to reveal the top of Ezra's short-haired widow's peak.

"*¡Entrá, rápido!*" he snapped.

Renata and Andrew ducked inside the shanty home. Ezra closed the door behind them. Words began to rush from Renata's mouth. "*Ezra, perdón por venir otra vez y a esta hora, pero estamos en problemas. Dijo el yanqui que—*"

Ezra shushed over her explanation for their unexpected visit. "*Vengan,*" he said and directed them to a small, circular table near a stocky cast-iron furnace in the rear of the dwelling. "*Tomen asiento,*" he said and motioned to the chairs. Andrew and Renata took a seat; Ezra took one opposite them. He rested his elbows on the table and tapped his fingers together, stewing in his thoughts. "*Parece haber mejorado mucho,*" he remarked, noting Andrew's improved condition. There was a tightness in his voice, and he did not blink. Andrew recollected Ezra's voice from last night but did not recognize his face.

"*Ezra, And-jru, el yanqui, dijo que los rufianes nos están buscando pero yo no lo creo. Es imposible, ¿no?*" she asked, injecting as much certainty into her voice as she could muster. Andrew knew she was relaying his warning. Ezra continued rolling his fingers across the table with his head in hand. He let out an exasperated sigh.

"*El yanqui tiene razón,*" Ezra said.

His words affirming Andrew's fears made Renata's jaw clench. She took in a deep breath through her nostrils and held it. With her response, Andrew strove to compose himself. "*¿Cómo sabés eso?*" Her voice fluttered as she asked why Ezra agreed. She sat with her hands compressed in her lap. She needed Ezra to assure her. He started with levity, stating that he wished Andrew had killed their attacker from last night, but his tone became severe when he started explaining how the ruffians had described the three of them when they put out a bounty for them. As Danuta was one of the prostitutes under their charge, they had an accurate description of her. Renata attempted to interject, but Ezra put a hand up and assured her that Danuta was fine; he had found a suitable family for her to stay with, far from the city.

Renata closed her eyes and released the grip around her lungs. "*Gracias a Dios que está a salvo,*" she said and made the *señal de la cruz*. In regards to Renata, the ruffians had loose descriptions but nothing concrete. They knew of Andrew the "*yanqui*" on account of his accent but had no specifics on his appearance. They sat in silence for a moment after Ezra finished. Renata stared at him, tapping her thumbs, stewing in thought. "*¿Qué podemos hacer?*" She asked Ezra what they could do. "*No tenemos dónde ir.*"

"*¿Tus padres?*" replied Ezra, suggesting they stay at her parents' place again. "*¿No pueden quedarse con ellos de nuevo?*"

Renata dropped her eyes and shook her head. She expressed concerns for the safety of her parents. She explained that another night would certainly infuriate them and they would banish her to exile with her aunt in the countryside, rendering her useless to the cause. Ezra assured her she was an invaluable asset, and he could not lose her. Her pupils widened. She asked Ezra if they could stay at the safe house. Ezra promptly denied the request, recapitulating his reasons from the night before, and the heightened risks since. Renata leaned over the table and deferred to Ezra for a solution. He rested his chin against his fist and paused. Andrew and Renata stared at him as he twisted his lips around an array of ideas. Outside, a busker churned his *bandoneón*. Its concertina sound hummed into the safehouse, seemingly triggering something inside of Ezra. He lowered his hand and nodded to himself, then floated the idea of taking refuge in a park café on the northern side of the capital, one he called "Café de Hansen."

"*¿Lo de Hansen?*" exclaimed Renata. She stood up to condemn the notion, though Ezra appeared complacent. "*¡Es una milonga!*"

The *milongas* were dance halls where illicit dancing and sordid fraternization occurred. Buenos Aires' elites publicly deemed such places repugnant to the high-toned atmosphere of the city, though they patronized *Lo de Hansen* and privately capitalized on such hives for nefarious dealings when legal means failed. Ezra's position was that it was a café—not a *milonga*. This made Renata's anger bubble. They both knew quite well that, by day, Hansen's posed as a refined café where little girls and their mothers wearing lace gloves shared teacakes. But when the sun went down, it transformed into the kind of *milonga* she detested. And he seemed to believe that since Renata frequented brothels, she had no reason to be so offended at this suggestion. Ezra's coyness about this displeased her; they both knew her missions required her to visit such establishments, and she said as much.

In turn, this pleased Ezra, for he also suggested this as a mission: stay at Café de Hansen until the danger subsides.

Renata had heated her forehead from rubbing it so much as she sighed and wrestled with the idea. She asked Ezra how he knew Café de Hansen would be safe. He explained that he had known the original German owner, Johan Hansen, who passed away a few years ago. Johan had owed Ezra a great debt that Ezra never redeemed, but he believed the current owner, Sebastián Monsch, would hold true to Johan's word. Ezra told Renata that she and Andrew must seek him out. This did not convince Renata, who feared the trip there might merely make things worse by exposing them to view. Ezra remained optimistic, insisting that Café de Hansen was one of the few places outside of the ruffians' control. Renata let out a groan of defeat and sat back in her chair. She rolled her head along the top of the backrest towards Andrew and peered up at him wearily.

"Tenemos un largo paseo, Yanqui," she said. By her tone, Andrew gathered they were in for another long night.

Chapter 9

Ezra unfurled a map of Buenos Aires. It had markings showing various brothels, pubs, inns, and safe houses across the city. He pointed to their location in La Boca, then glided his finger to a green splotch northward labeled *Parque 3 de Febrero*. The green splotch denoted a park. Within it was a tiny black dot for the café. It sat near the top of the map, just below the wide blue streak marked Río de la Plata, the "River of Silver." Based on the map scale, the café was about five miles from their current position.

"Here you must go: Café Hansen," stated Ezra in clunky English to Andrew. "You cannot enter in Puerto Madero. They search for you." He pointed to the four light blue rectangles on the east side. "Also, here," he added. Ezra had his finger on a street called *Junin*. "Do not enter also. Stay away, yeah?" Andrew studied the map and nodded. Once everyone seemed satisfied, Ezra led them to the door. Renata knotted her shawl, and Andrew fixed his cap. *"Cuídense,"* Ezra whispered before closing the door.

Andrew stared back at the door where Ezra, a moment before, had wished them safe travels.

"Dale, Yanqui," said Renata, insisting they get going.

They turned the corner and headed north. Crowds started

to appear: townsfolk romping toward their destinations in packs, or hunkering down in chatty groups. Andrew walked in tandem with Renata but keeping a step behind. Her short legs maximized their stride, with crossed arms nestled beneath her shawl. Andrew pulled out his pack of hand-rolled cigarettes and tapped one out. He struck a match, lit the end, and puffed until the tobacco flared.

"*Por favor, apague esa luz. No soporto el olor,*" said Renata. She had her hand over her nose and mouth.

"You—you want me to put it out?" Andrew asked, holding up the cigarette.

"*Sí, por favor.*"

Andrew looked at her, then shrugged. He took a long final drag before flicking it into the street. Renata smiled at him, appreciating the gesture. Its stench departed, only for the breeze to introduce the delectable smells of street gastronomy. Renata took in a whiff.

"*Mmm, tengo hambre. ¿Y vos?*" she asked.

"Um, *qué?*" Andrew replied.

"*Tengo hambre.*" She placed her hand on her stomach and rubbed it.

"Oh, you're hungry. Me too; *shoh, tahm-bee-en,*" Andrew said, pointing at himself with a wry grin. Renata's diaphragm tightened, forcing an airy giggle.

"*¿Querés algo de comer?*" she asked. She pointed over her shoulder to a busy street vendor's grill, or *parrilla*.

"Oh, um, *sí.* Me—*may goo-stah,* um, *al-go* to *co-mare.*"

"*Vení.*"

At the parilla, locals called out their orders. An elderly couple stood behind the grill, tending to the fare. The man hovered over the encrusted grates suspended over a coal fire. He tossed a mixture of seasoned beef, onions, and peppers on one side of the grill. The woman worked next to him, taking round discs of flour dough and scooping some of the mixture into them. She folded the discs in half over the filling and crimped the edges, forming half-moon-shaped meat pies. She slid them to the other side of the parrilla, where the man took his spatula and maneuvered them next to a row of other, browning ones. He flipped a few to cook the opposite side before again attending to the meat blend on the pan.

"*Empanadas,*" Renata stated proudly.

"*Em-puh-nadas,*" Andrew repeated.

"*Sí,*"

"They look good."

A couple of the locals turned to look at the English speaker. Renata grabbed Andrew's arm and stared at him. She pressed a finger to her lips and shook her head. Andrew locked his mouth with a pretend key. The couple at the empanada stand handed out the meat pies in wrapped newspaper to each customer. Everyone seemed familiar and exchanged pleasantries with the woman, giving her some coin and a *beso en la mejilla* before departing. When it was their turn, Andrew and Renata stepped forth.

"Renata," chimed the old woman. She had a cheery scratch to her voice.

"*Buenas noches, Señora Biancolin,*" said Renata. "*¿Cómo está?*"

With pleasantries exchanged, Señora Biancolin felt compelled to ask what a woman like her was doing out at such an hour. Many saw this as unbecoming. Renata admitted that she could not resist one of the Biancolins' famous empanadas and had to see her. The old woman assured her there was no sin in that. When she caught sight of Andrew over Renata's shoulder, she lowered her voice and noted he looked like a foreign sailor, remarking on his imposing frame yet reserved nature. She was clearly curious about his relationship with Renata. Renata assured her he was just a befriended traveler accompanying her and, with tactful speed, redirected the conversation towards the empanadas. Señora Biancolin asked Renata how many she would like.

"*Cuatro, por favor,*" said Renata. Señor Biancolin swiped four of the done empanadas into an open sheet of newspaper and loosely wrapped them. Renata withdrew some coins and dropped them into Señora Biancolin's hand.

"*Muchas gracias,*" said Renata.

"*De nada,*" replied Señora Biancolin. "*Decile a tu madre que la voy a ver en la misa.*"

"*¡Se lo voy a decir!*"

Renata kissed the woman on the cheek, and they resumed their trek northward. She unfurled the newspaper and handed one of the empanadas to Andrew, who juggled it from hand to hand until his palms could bear its heat. He took a bite. He winced and tongued the food around in his mouth and emitted a gargled, huffing sound from the back of his throat.

"*Tené paciencia,*" she pleaded, warning him to wait.

Andrew disgorged the piece of piping hot empanada into his palm. He looked at Renata. She giggled, her fingers covering her mouth.

"*Una bestia,*" she said, alluding to his "beast"-like behavior. She let out a snort and laughed harder.

"I hope you are quite satisfied. I'll wait," said Andrew.

"*¡Basta! Basta, Renata,*" she ordered herself. Once composed, she looked up at Andrew.

"*Ahora come la empanada en un bocado.*" She motioned with

her hands for Andrew to put the gooey piece of the mushed meat pastry back into his mouth. Andrew flung it in like a shot of cheap liquor. The sharp flavors of beef and pepper struck him—rich with taste and hearty spices. The pie's beige and auburn crust had a savory crunch.

"Lord, that hits the spot," he remarked.

Renata nodded, pleased with herself. She bit off a corner of the pie and munched it with a broad smile.

"*¡Mmm! Iguales a las que hace mi mamá,*" she said.

"Your mom, *tu madre,* makes these?" Andrew asked.

Renata nodded. They looked at each other. Neither spoke the other's language but felt more connected than seemed conceivable. They smiled until bashfulness overtook their gazes.

They continued northward through La Boca with empanadas in hand and gullet. Renata kept them on the west side of the barrio. They entered Barracas and arrived under a streetlight near La Gruta de Plaza Constitución, a dilapidated castle-like structure on Lima Street, strangled by vines and foliage. Andrew tapped her on the shoulder with the dictionary:

How much—Cuánto

Longer—Largo

Do—Hacer

We—Nosotros

Have—Tener

Renata pressed her thumb and fingers together in a questioning upwards gesture like a cone, giving him a puzzled look. "*¿Cuánto largo hacer tenemos?*" she said.

"*Ah la rest-oo-rahntay dae* Hansen's," he said slowly.

"Ahh," she exclaimed. "*Una hora.*" She made a circle with her fingers, mimicking the minute hand on a clock.

"Still an hour?" he said, holding up one finger.

Renata bobbed her head and nodded. Andrew grumbled as a horse and buggy came alongside them. Without notice, Andrew jogged after it and flagged down the driver. Renata chased after him.

"*¿Poo-edo oo-sar tu,* um, carriage?" he asked the driver. The driver looked at him funny and quizzically held up a hand with pinched fingers.

Renata caught up and asked Andrew, "*¿Qué hacés? No podemos permitírnoslo.*" She raised her hand and rubbed the inside of her index finger and thumb together.

Andrew pulled a few coins from his peacoat and showed them to her. "How far can this get us?" he asked.

She was prepared with an objection until she saw his silvery palm. It was enough to get them to any point in the city proper by coach. Her feet had started to ache and blister. She knew the longer they remained on the streets, the chances of the ruffians finding them only increased.

"*¿Podría llevarnos a Café Hansen en Parque 3 de Febrero?*" she asked.

The driver placed his buggy whip and top hat in his lap and leaned forward to study the pair.

"*Podría llevarte allá, pero primero voy a tener que ver el pago,*" said the driver.

Renata reached for Andrew's wrist and hoisted it up to the driver to show they had the means. He looked at the coins in Andrew's palm, sifted through them, and plucked the necessary compensation.

"*Subir a bordo,*" he announced. The coachman stepped down from the driver's seat and opened the door. He lent a hand to the lady, guiding Renata into the buggy. Andrew hoisted himself into the space next to her. She tucked her lower lip between her teeth, trying to stifle her excitement. Taking a carriage felt grand to her. She nestled into the button-tufted leather seat, and the coachman flicked the reins. The buggy lurched forward, and Renata laced her arms around Andrew's bicep, pressing her cheek against his shoulder. She froze. Realizing her impropriety, she turned her eyes up at Andrew. She wanted to brace herself against his frame. It steadied her nerves, and she felt safe. Andrew nodded.

"*¡Nunca antes había estado en una calesa!*" she admitted excitedly.

"*No en-tee-en-doe,* I don't understand," Andrew replied.

The coachman could not help but chuckle, and Renata and Andrew did so along with him. She asked Andrew for the dictionary and, using the faint orange glow from the passing street lamps, read her translation.

"Never beh-fore I been een dees," she managed to utter.

"You've never been in one of these before? In a carriage, *sí?*"

"Yes," she replied with an exasperated sigh. "*No sé cómo podés hablar así.*"

Andrew laughed and took back the dictionary. "*Sho, sen-teer, el mies-mo,*" he replied.

Renata asked for the dictionary. "We cahn prr-ac-teez toh-ged-er."

"I like it. *Mae goostuh eh-so.*"

Andrew and Renata continued swapping the dictionary like schoolchildren as the carriage rolled through Lima Street. Each took turns translating, through sheepish smiles. Grammar was at the rear, and laughter was at the front. They kept the phrases simple and pointed to the sights and objects along the way:

"*Noche,*" she said.

"Night," he replied.

"*Caballo.*"

"Horse."

"*Calle.*"

"Street."

The street lamps lit the way—brighter and brighter. They reached maximum radiancy when they entered Avenida de Mayo, where lampposts illuminated the way clear down its center. A sky full of possibilities, sealed by nightfall, encased the wonder of the city's eternal soul. Like a mirror to the stars, the city's glow accented the brilliance of this human masterpiece. The carriage travelers fell victim to the splendor and elegance of Buenos Aires, entranced by its singular beauty. Renata gripped Andrew's arm tighter.

"Plaza de Mayo," she exclaimed. Her finger pointed east.

"*¡La Caw-saw Row-saw-daw!* I saw it," Andrew added, pointing at the silhouette of the distant palace.

"*¡Mira vos!*" she said with surprise. She then pointed west as they crossed the center of the bustling intersection.

"Plaza Lorea."

"Ahh," Andrew replied. In the moonlight, he made out a boxy-shaped tower looming in the distance.

"Well, I'll be damned. They do have Mr. Eiffel's Tower. I'll have to tell Vince this really is Paris," he said.

Renata let out a giggle. "*Sí, si te referís al tanque de agua del Señor Eiffel.*"

"Ahh, *tahn-kay de ah-gwah.* So it is a tank of water—or a water tank—a water tower. It's 'Paris' enough for me!"

Renata leaned into him. "We are, um, how chu sae—*barato París,*" she said.

They entered Cerrito Street, out from the city's central artery.

The streets seemed wider and the crowds thinner. Andrew felt Renata nestle herself deeper into his arm and relax her grip. He watched her eyes flash in the lamplight and felt something sweet for her. They passed a park with a single statue, the Plaza Libertad. Three blocks more, they reached the intersection where Cerrito met Juncal. The driver angled the reins, and the carriage yawed left.

"Cinco Esquinas," muttered Renata.

"*Cinco;* five. Five what?" asked Andrew.

"*Esquinas,*" she repeated, tapping the tips of her index fingers together to make a point.

"Fingers; *es-kee-naws* means fingers?"

"*Sí,*" she said, pointing to the northwest road, Avenida República, then to Libertad, running perpendicular to Juncal.

"Oh, five points," Andrew exclaimed. "Like the one in Manhattan."

They came by a street sign with the word Junin on it. Andrew turned to Renata. She motioned him to keep quiet. Andrew tilted the brim of his cap down. He noticed a few folks getting out of carriages at the tramway station they were passing by, but nothing unusual. Renata also seemed content, for she motioned to a fence of iron bars just ahead, encompassing a crowded collection of ornate mausoleums.

"Cementerio de la Recoleta," she said. She pointed to a colonial-era basilica on the far side of the cemetery. "Iglesia del Pilar." The forest of gothic tombs sat silently beneath their belfry guard.

"Haunting," Andrew remarked.

They bumped over some railroad tracks on Avenida General Las Heras, then up to Bustamante, and diverted right. The street cut short and fed into Avenida Alvear. The road doubled, even tripled, in width, and before them flowed a pilgrimage of carriages guided by the glowing lampposts down the avenue. Palms, rosewoods, and jacarandas displaced the stone grandeur that had earlier lined their voyage. A pale moon emitted hazy light in the dark heavens, and slowly the sounds of the city eased, the hoofbeats of the horses ceased to echo, and crickets chirped out of time Andrew and Renata soaked in the stillness of the night.

"Say, you think they are all going to Hansen's?" Andrew asked of the carriages ahead.

"*Estoy segura que sí,*" Renata affirmed, nodding.

They followed the eastward herd as the road transitioned to Avenida de Buenos Aires, where the foliage thickened along the riverside. The carriages, running wheel-to-wheel, banked right at the French fountain in the intersection. The equine teams whinnied and chomped at one another. Passengers gawked and pointed at the imposing nearby military college that not long ago had been the estate of a bloodthirsty general. A new stone gateway contributed to the traffic jam, forcing the side-by-side carriages to squeeze through its pillars. The coachmen barked and cursed through the *portones*. Once free, Andrew and Renata's carriage went on ahead on Avenida de las Palmeras, Avenue of the Palms, christened for its stately, overarching palm trees. A beckoning glow and music drifting from the establishment ahead guided them forward. The flock of carriages veered towards it over the train tracks and through the trees.

"*Llegamos. Café de Hansen,*" announced the driver.

Chapter 10

The rectangular, cream-colored structure was fit for a Spanish royal's garden party. Vines of dead wisteria slunk through the adjoined pergola out front, and delicate white tiling covered the floors. Just below the balustrade lining the roof, a sign proclaimed it the Restaurante del Parque 3 de Febrero. A small inscription on the opposite side displayed the name "J. Hansen." The carriages scarred the soil with their wheels as top hats and shiny dresses spilled out of them. The entranced patrons shambled towards the sparkle and sound pulsating from within the restaurant.

The driver hopped down from his seat and pulled open the door. Andrew stepped out and guided Renata down the folding step. He went to tip the coachman, but the man declined the offer with a smile.

"That was awfully nice of him," remarked Andrew as the driver sped off.

"*¡Vamos!*" said Renata.

She grabbed Andrew by the hand and led him to a sweaty footman dressed in a fine black suit. The man was endeavoring to shepherd the throng through the packed doors, with little success.

"*¡Disculpe!*" shouted Renata to the footman, who continued

to direct traffic while stepping towards Renata.

"*Sí, ¿puedo ayudarle?*" he shouted back.

"*¿Sabe dónde podemos encontrar a Sebastián Monsch?*"

"*¿Señor Monsch, quién pregunta por él?*"

"*Dígale que Ezra Rachman nos envió,*" she replied with apprehension.

The footman lifted an eyebrow and studied her before giving himself a reassuring nod. "*Entendido, por favor, espere acá,*" he said, then darted off. The footman appeared relieved to have a reason to leave his post. Renata looked at Andrew with a dimpled grin. They waited and watched the crowd shuffling in. Several minutes passed before the footman returned.

"*Por acá, por favor,*" he urged Renata and Andrew.

They followed him into the café, brimming with guests who had packed themselves around marble tables. Music from the band bounced at a feverish pace, and the central chamber's floor bobbed with illicit dancers. It was apparent the place drew patrons with a rhapsody of vices: stiff liquors, imported cigars, high-stake card games, and keen heiresses. It was a place where Buenos Aires' high society reveled in debauchery and sin, free from retributive laws and the officials they had bought and paid for.

The footman led them around the edge of the dance hall and into a corridor, off which were several private rooms. They approached one of the doors, and the footman knocked.

"*¡Se abre!*" shouted a voice on the other side.

The footman twisted the knob and gestured for Andrew and Renata to enter. They stepped into a drawing room sizable enough for a small gathering. The few candles gave off scraps of light, but the blaze from the exterior lampposts through the window pane kept the room aglow. At the back, facing the window, a man stood staring out.

"*Señor Monsch, estas son las personas que lo solicitan en nombre de—*"

The mysterious figure raised his hand. "*Gracias, Pablo. Esto será todo,*" he replied.

"*Sí, señor,*" said the footman. He stepped out and shut the door behind them. The man took a sip from the lowball glass in his hand and set it down. Then he approached Andrew and Renata, bearing a cheery smile. His straightened back and stiff shoulders gave him an air of distinction and propriety.

"*Buenas noches, me presento formalmente, soy el Señor Monsch, propietario de este establecimiento,*" he said with a genteel bow.

"*Buenas noches, señor. Un gusto conocerle,*" said Renata. Señor Monsch extended his hand, and Renata placed hers in it. He pressed her knuckles up to his lips, then reached for Andrew's in the form of a handshake.

"*Bwhen-ahs no-chess, señor,*" said Andrew.

Señor Monsch paused and lifted his finger at Andrew. "*Usted,* um, chu—you are American?" he sputtered.

"Yes, sir. I am," Andrew replied, surprised.

The man nodded to himself. "I know a leet-el Een-glesh," he said.

Andrew gave him a grin, which was followed by an awkward silence.

"*Antes de que el Señor Hansen muriera,*" started Señor Monsch, "*me dio una lista de nombres;* he gave me names. *Nombres que me dijo;* he told me: '*Sebastián, pase lo que pase,* no matter what, *cualquiera en esta lista,* in this list of the names, *que necesite ayuda debe dársela,* you must help them.' *En esa lista, solo hay cinco nombres,* just five names. *Uno de ellos es Ezra Rachman.*" The man glanced from one to the other with somber eyes. "*Bueno, no necesito saber sus nombres ni cómo conocen al Señor Rachman, pero les voy a ayudar de cualquier manera que pueda;* I will help you no matter the circumstances."

"*Gracias, señor,*" said Renata.

"Yes, thank you," added Andrew.

"*Ahora, ¿cómo puedo ser de serles de ayuda?* How can I help?" Señor Monsch asked.

"*Estamos un poco en problemas,*" admitted Renata.

"Trouble, what kind? *¿Qué tipo de problemas?*"

"*Los rufianes: usted sabe de quiénes le hablo—nos están buscando y necesitamos un lugar para pasar la noche. Esperábamos poder quedarnos acá.*"

Señor Monsch stared at her pensively. He took a moment to assess Andrew and Renata's predicament and the suggested solution of using his establishment as a hideout. He pursed his lips and nodded.

"*Entonces, ustedes deben ser las dos personas que ellos están buscando, señorita.* You the ones they are looking for," remarked Señor Monsch. Renata attempted to plead her case, but Señor Monsch put a hand up.

"I am familiar with Señor Rachman's *cómo diría,* 'work.' It's noble, *y espero que algún día encuentre a su querida hermana.*"

Renata nodded. Señor Monsch then proceeded to the back of the parlor and poured a dram of whiskey from the carafe into the lowball glass.

"You may stay; *pueden quedarse acá,*" he declared before sipping his glass.

"*Muchas gracias, Señor Monsch. Le estaríamos enormemente agradecidos,*" Renata expressed her gratitude emphatically.

"We truly appreciate it," added Andrew.

"*Pero tengan cuidado,*" he continued. "*Estos hombres son*

peligrosos; they are dangerous men. *Aconsejo que nunca vuelvas a jugar con ellos.*"

"We understand," said Andrew.

"*Sí, comprendemos,*" added Renata.

"*Muy bien,*" said Señor Monsch, bringing some levity into his voice. "*Entonces, haré que uno de mis hombres, Gerardo, prepare dos habitaciónes para ustedes.* He speaks English too. *¿Les parece bien?*"

Andrew looked at Renata.

"*Sí, señor,*" she replied. "*Es perfecto.*"

"*¡Espléndido!* Please; *por favor, disfruten de la comida y bebidas,* enjoy the food and drink, *de forma gratuita;* all for free. *Sus habitaciones no estarán listas hasta que yo termine.*"

Andrew and Renata thanked Señor Monsch again before he showed them out of the room. Together they climbed a nearby flight of stairs to a private table overlooking the dance hall. Andrew pulled out one of the chairs beside the railing for Renata. Her face went red; she had never been treated as a formal guest in this way, much less found herself swimming in the midst of so much splendor and wealth.

"I will send for Gerardo," announced Señor Monsch.

"Thank you, sir," Andrew replied.

He took the seat across from Renata and watched her over the paraffin lamp as she surveyed the scene below, her eyes wide. She turned towards Andrew and shook her head.

"*¿Qué?*" Andrew asked, the corner of his lip turning up in amusement.

Renata pulled the dictionary out. She spoke as she flipped to each appropriate page.

"My parents no bul-eev th-ees," she said with a nervous giggle.

Andrew laughed. "*Yo también.*"

She forced a smile, but it slumped.

"*¿Qué?*" asked Andrew again, repeating the reliable word.

Renata twisted her mouth. "I cah-n't go bah-ck to my pah-rents."

"You can't go back? *¿Por qué?*"

Through broken English, they endeavored to comprehend one another. She told him about her life. From what he gathered, she was a second-generation Argentine from an Italian family; her father was a bricklayer and her mother tended to the home. Renata had found living with her mother a strain and took the first job she could. She worked as a cigarette roller for a tobacco company called La Abundancia. She loathed the tedious and ceaseless labor and smell of the factory. It was through a coworker that she had come to meet Ezra Rachman.

Ezra came from a poor Jewish family in a village outside Warsaw. During his time in Poland, antisemitic riots plagued the land, and Polish Jewish families, such as Ezra's, lived in constant trepidation. Ezra's only sister was the first of the family to seek a better life when she responded to an advertisement by the Varsovia Jewish Mutual Aid Society posted at the family's local synagogue. It promised young girls and women employment as house servants for wealthy Jewish families within the Buenos Aires region. The advertisers provided the transportation, and his sister left shortly thereafter. Many women and girls followed. Months passed before Ezra's family received word from her. It came in the form of a note scratched on a piece of hotel stationery. Ezra's sister explained the ruffians had taken her and forced her into slavery—the kind where men paid for the carnal taste of broken and helpless youth. The ruffians—Polish Jews who also immigrated to Argentina—came with dreams of enterprise, profiting from the exploitation of the conscripted girls under the guise of a mutual aid society.

Ezra left for Argentina as soon as possible and promised never to return to Poland without her. When he arrived in Puerto Madero, he had little money. Ezra's will and determination to find his sister led him to cultivate a network of allies, supporters, and volunteers who were also keen to liberate these women. On the outside, Ezra seemed like a selfless hero, working in the shadows to counter the ruffians; in reality, all of this was a means to find his sister and bring her back to Warsaw. He had yet to find her, with only whispers to show for his efforts. Renata feared she was already dead, but neither she nor anyone else would indulge such a notion. Ezra's efforts had freed countless women, giving them new lives with families far from Buenos Aires and outside of the ruffians' reach. Without Ezra, the entire operation would crumble.

Renata had begun working for Ezra about six months previous, earning a few pesos by performing minor jobs such as surveying or reporting the ruffians' routines and movements. This led to Ezra entrusting her with more perilous assignments, such as rescue missions or infiltrating ruffian strongholds such as El Nacional. She had found purpose in her work and wanted to continue it, so, unbeknownst to her parents, she had quit her job at the tobacco company and dedicated her time solely to this cause. Nevertheless, her mother had grown suspicious of her clandestine lifestyle.

"*¿Qué, vahn, a, hacer a ti?*" he asked.

Renata dropped her eyes and shook her head. "*Mi mamá*, has plan *para* me go."

"Your mother has plans for you to go, as in go away?"

"*Sí, pero me voy a negar. Prefiero vivir en la calle,*" she added defiantly.

Andrew understood: she would refuse to leave Buenos Aires. She was braver and brighter than most people he knew, and he admired her for it. With the joy glittering on the dance floor below them, Andrew felt guilty about prying. Fear had put a huge strain on him since the night of the attack, and he knew she must feel a similar weight, if not a heavier one.

"Hey," Andrew said. He took the dictionary, fumbled through the pages, and attempted to express his admiration for her. "*Vos, uh, vos sos va-she-yente,*" he said. "*Or-gew-sho-so.*"

Renata gave an embarrassed grin. "*Gracias,*" she replied. They smiled at one another. He felt a complete desire for her. A split-second reverie crossed his mind; he pondered smuggling her aboard *Dismal Queen* and back to the United States. He had never met a girl—in this hemisphere or his own—like her.

A *mesero* approached their table, relieving Andrew of the thought. The waiter sported a dark handlebar mustache, slicked-back hair, and a crisp tuxedo, like the rest of the waitstaff.

"Good evening," he said. "*Soy Gerardo,* and I will be your server tonight. Señor Monsch informs me that you speak English, yes?" he asked, looking at Andrew.

"Yes. How do you do, *Hare—Hare—Hare-rard-row*?" Andrew replied.

"Gerard is fine if it pleases you, *señor*," he said. "I am happy to, eh, practice my English."

"It's a relief," said Andrew. "Where did you learn?"

"My mother, she is Canadian, but my father is *argentino.*"

"Canadian, you say. I'd be surprised if you didn't know French as well."

"*Je connais le français,*" he stated proudly.

"Well, I'll be damned!" said Andrew. "You're one-of-a-kind, Gerard-o."

"Thank you, *señor.* Señor Monsch would like to offer one of his finest imported bottles of vintage Moët & Chandon. Would that interest you both?"

Andrew looked at Renata. "Champagne?" he asked. Renata shrugged. "Sounds good to us."

"*Bueno,*" said the waiter. "Anything to eat, or perhaps a *picada* will suffice."

"*Uh, una picada,*" exclaimed Renata.

Andrew laughed. "I guess we will have *dos picadas* then." Andrew held two fingers up.

"*No, no, no,*" interjected Renata. "*Vamos a tener solo una picada.*" She put up one finger. "*Él no entiende.*"

"*Por supuesto, señorita,*" Gerardo said with a chuckle. "*La picada estará lista para que ustedes la disfruten durante el espectáculo.*"

"*¿Espectáculo?*" repeated Renata.

"I know that one; it means 'spectacle,'" piped in Andrew.

"Very good, *señor,*" said the waiter. "Yes, tonight, we will have two of the finest *tango* dancers performing."

"Sounds intriguing. But, what is *tahn-go* dancing, anyway?"

"Tango is a dance that some may say is a bit … provocative and surely forbidden in Buenos Aires. Of course, here, in *Lo de Hansen,* we welcome and permit all forms of … culture."

"I see."

Gerardo gave a wry grin. "Just wait, *señor.* I'm sure it will be like nothing you've ever seen before."

The band stopped and finished with a splashy coda. Everyone clapped and gabbed with verve. Andrew and Renata watched from above as a master of ceremonies took the floor, waving his hands.

"*¡Atención! ¡Atención, por favor!*" shouted the man.

The crowd quieted, and the staff shuffled from table to table to douse the lanterns. The volume fell to a decibel below the rumble of the carriages outside. The man started by telling a story with amusing bravado. He rambled about a magical flower that fell from a tree in the Amazon and drifted hundreds of miles south down a river. During its travel, it witnessed the dances of the indigenous tribes and the skillful courtship and movements of the exotic birds and beasts before scuttling upon the shores of the Río de la Plata. From there, a woman of great beauty sprang from the blossom, possessing the uncanny ability to dance the tango. Although he did not understand a word, Andrew enjoyed the tone and boisterous spirit of the storyteller. Renata stretched her neck over the railing.

"*¡Sin más preámbulos,*" belted the orator, "*Permítanme presentarles, el pétalo escarlata del Amazonas, Corola, dirigido por el talentoso Valentino Pérez!*"

As the master of ceremonies finished, he gestured to one of the corridors leading to the private rooms. There appeared the lady of the Amazonian blossom, Corola, accompanied by the gentleman, Señor Pérez. They made their way to the dance floor. She had caramel skin, blistering red lipstick, and sleek nightshade hair pinned behind her head, fitted with a carmine-colored flower. Her side-slitted dress matched her lips. It hugged her sinewy figure and extended down to the middle of her calf. The crowd murmured and stirred as they surveyed her bare collarbones, midriff, and peeking thighs. Señor Pérez wore a tame charcoal suit. He had a square jawline and a fair-skinned, handsome face with jet-black hair greased back, like most young men in Buenos Aires.

The light of the chandelier shined over them through a

cigarette haze, and the mirrors along the walls made the room seem like endless halls of luminaries. The pair positioned themselves counter to the other at the center of the floor. Shushes silenced the chatter, and the room went still. The bandoneon breathed, and the piano struck its chord, sounding the charge. Señor Pérez strutted toward her with sharp eyes, holding out a sturdy left hand for her to take. She received it, and he pressed the small of her back with his right. She nestled her hand into his and placed her other on his shoulder. They leaned into one another, her lips inches from his collar. The bass and violin joined the procession with a charming tune of a suggestive brew.

Señor Pérez traced his foot against the floor. He moved it to and fro from her, staging the tempo. Corola mirrored his movements. Then they started to shuffle: side-to-side, front-to-back, knees intertwined like vines. At each half-note, they paused, winding up before the eighth-note commenced, then releasing an array of prances and pivots in and out and beneath the other. It appeared more like a challenge than a dance as each step, twist, and turn tested the other's ability to match the alternating rhythm and cadence.

Corola's hips snapped and swiveled from one side of Señor Pérez and back to the other as he led her about. The melody churned faster, and the motions became more deft and rapid. In one motion, Corola threw her back into Señor Pérez, who slung her up and across his torso like a sash and twirled her for all to see. She wrapped her high heels around his leg and her arm over his shoulder. With a snap, the lady unraveled to the floor. Renata jumped from her seat, certain the dancer would slam into the floor. Instead, she glided downward, thanks to the adroitness of Señor Pérez. He breathed into her exposed neck, then guided her back to her feet and into their starting positions. They continued their writhing and twisting, extravagant and true to the myth of the tango. When the finale came, Señor Pérez extended Corola above his head. The violin and concertinas laid their final note, and she fell into him with a submissive embrace.

The slack-jawed onlookers clapped and cheered. Corola and Señor Pérez gave a short bow and thanked them. One of the spectators handed Corola a rose, which she accepted with a curtsy. The performers waved at their admirers and departed the floor, to a roar of adulation.

Andrew found Renata tucked neatly against his frame. She had edged herself closer to him throughout the spectacle. "You all right?" he asked. Renata, realizing she had invaded his personal space, peered up at him.

"*Sí,*" she admitted, sounding content. Andrew looked upon her. He wanted to burn the moment into his mind: Her hair draped over her defined, yet soft Italian complexion, and the warm glow of the candlelight dazzling her seraphic eyes. She let him study her until timidity caused her cheeks to redden. She set her hair back and turned towards the table. Two fizzing champagne glasses stood next to the *picada.* She looked back at him with a devilish grin and motioned with her head at the table. Andrew smiled and bobbed his eyebrows.

"Do you wanna …" he asked, leaning towards the food and drink.

"*Sí,*" she said.

They touched glasses. Andrew slugged down the coupe; Renata gave credence to the flavors. They then dove into the picada: a large wooden platter displaying heaps of salami, manchego, mortadella, Spanish *jamón,* seasoned roasted peppers, black olives, green olives, pine nuts, walnuts, peanuts, provoleta, reggianito, prosciutto, blood sausage, half a baguette, and salted crackers.

Renata explained, in hasty Spanish, the different cuts and cheeses as she plunged a sample of each of them into Andrew's mouth. Andrew nodded, gauging her opinion of each by the tone she used. At one point, he struggled to lap up a piece of mortadella that drooped from his mouth like a dog's tongue, sending them into side-splitting laughter. They dined in gluttonous surrender. Scraps littered the plate when the clock struck midnight. Andrew looked at Renata, who was beaming with contentment.

"I am—how do you say 'stuffed' in Spanish?" he asked, patting his belly. Renata giggled.

"*Lleno,*" she replied. "*Estoy lleno.*"

"*Estoy shen-o,*" he repeated. He leaned back in his chair and caught sight of Gerardo climbing the stairs with a bottle of champagne in hand. "But not too '*shen-o*' for a nightcap." Andrew waved for Gerardo. The *masero* approached their table and tilted the bottle into Renata's glass. As the glass filled, he leaned over and whispered something into her ear. Her pupils shrank, and the color disappeared from her face.

"What? What's going on?" Andrew asked.

Gerardo stepped towards Andrew, leaned into his ear, and poured his drink. "*Señor,* I regret to inform you that you will not be able to stay here tonight. The ruffians searching for you—they are here."

Chapter 11

A shiver crawled down Andrew's spine. He looked up at Gerardo. "They are here, now, in the café?!"

"I'm afraid so," replied Gerardo.

Andrew took a moment to process. He looked at Renata. She stared at him with her lips apart and an expression that begged the question, "What do we do?" He mustered his composure and dabbed his lip with a napkin. "Where are they?" he asked Gerardo.

The server continued his duties, tidying the table, diverting his eyes. "Across the room, first floor," he replied. Andrew eased against the backrest and peeked over the banister. "With discretion, *señor.*"

Andrew gave a stiff nod as he scanned the room. Café Hansen remained in its jovial state, as frenzied as a beehive. Dancers courted with their partners, and patrons buzzed from one table to the next, spreading gossip and influence. Nothing seemed distinguishable except for the ostensible queen bee Corola in her red dress, swarmed by male attendants. Andrew feigned an itch on the back of his neck to turn his head further. He spotted a table of hard-faced men from the corner of his eye. Six sat at the table; two stood over it like watchdogs. One of the men had a swollen and bandaged face. The purple and black shading distended so far as to render his left eye shut. Andrew was sure it was them.

"Do they know we are here?" he asked Gerardo.

"I don't know, *señor*," he replied. "Señor Monsch has instructed me to lead you safely out the back. I'll go ahead and make sure that all is clear. Then, I will return and lead you out. You will need to go on foot. I believe one of them is out front, minding the coaches."

"Can Señor Monsch ask them to leave?"

"I'm afraid not—not someone like them."

Andrew paused, then nodded. "All right, could you please tell the lady?"

"She already knows."

"Thank you."

"Of course, *señor*." Gerardo departed and attended to the other tables.

Renata sat tight to her chair with her fingers laced in her lap. They did not speak, waiting as though they were preparing to face a firing squad. Andrew fidgeted and glanced over the railing to see if the table of assumed ruffians stirred.

"*Basta,*" Renata hissed.

The sparkling sound of shattering glass split the white noise below. Andrew and Renata jerked their heads over the banister to see a man lying flat on his back, attempting to stave off an attacker. Another grabbed the assailant by the shoulders to tear him off, but then another jumped upon his back and sank the man under his weight. A fight ensued, and the crowd cleared the tables to make space for the scrabble and solidify bets on the outcome.

"*Psst!*" came a noise from the stairway. Andrew and Renata turned to see Gerardo's face poking out from it. He beckoned them to follow. Both shot to their feet and sped towards him. He led them down and through the corridor of private rooms, against the current of spectators heading to the ballroom. They reached the back door, which opened to the wraparound patio. Gerardo pulled the door open and peered through the opening.

"*Bien,*" he said. Renata gave him a cheek kiss. "*Cuídensen,* take care," he said. Andrew shook his hand, slipping him several pesos, and followed Renata through the door. Those outside had started receiving word of the altercation within and were peering through the windows. Andrew took Renata by the hand and they walked onto the grass.

They strode hard and sharp toward the first copse of trees. The air was crisp, and their hearts picked up in pace as they entered dense forest. They passed couples canoodling on picnic blankets and in hidden gazebos. It was a labyrinth of foliage. "*Para allá,*" Renata said, motioning toward a glimmer of streetlight through the thicket. They dashed for it until they reached the pavement of Avenida de Buenos Aires, just south of the military college. Andrew rolled his shoulders back to catch his breath. The parade of carriages had dwindled to but a few, and the sidewalks were lonely.

"Where to?" asked Andrew.

"Ezra," she said confidently.

"Ezra? *Ezra dee-say no.*"

"*Lo sé.*"

Andrew twisted his lips and shrugged his shoulders. "If you say so."

They made their way down the avenue briskly, peeking over their shoulders every so often. Their steps grew heavy and their shoulders relaxed as they neared the metropolitan area. They passed the Cementerio de la Recoleta, then crossed Junin and found themselves back amongst the glass and stone. Andrew pulled Renata to the side and braced himself against one of the buildings. He stretched his legs, and several crackling pops from his knees followed. Renata kneaded her calves with her thumbs.

"That was some place," he said, looking at her with a grin.

"*Sí*," she said with a breathy chuckle. Her breathing eased. The distant taps of nearing footsteps caught her ear. She was not going to think much of it. She debated whether to look and possibly rouse suspicion or continue massaging her legs and seem disinterested. In the end, something compelled her to look. About sixty paces away came two figures striding towards them. They did not converse nor seem to be going about their business but rather were bearing down on them with deliberate speed. Renata's heart started to race again.

"*Dale*," she said sternly, tugging at Andrew's wrist.

"Why? What's the—"

From a bent-over position, he turned to see what had caught Renata's eye. He ceased his protesting and took her hand. Neither looked back as the hollow echo of the footsteps grew louder and their cadence increased. Andrew and Renata reached an intersection and hugged the corner. The footsteps followed and proceeded to gain ground. The opening to an alleyway lay just ahead. In a split-second decision, Andrew pulled Renata into it.

"*¡¿Qué boludo?!*" she cried.

She attempted to yank her arm in the opposite direction, but Andrew's strength overruled her. He realized his mistake when they stepped into the murky passage with no end in sight. It was too late to turn around; the footsteps were mere feet from them. Andrew and Renata splashed through stagnant puddles and stumbled over shards of broken bottles and splintered boards. Andrew glanced back to see a silhouette of a man standing at the mouth of the alley. A flash came from it, followed by an earsplitting bang. The whir of a bullet passed between Andrew and Renata, and a wall beyond spat slivers of brick.

"Run!" Andrew cried. He clutched Renata's hand with vise-like strength, and they broke out into a sprint. The gun roared thrice, each shot slipping past them. They heard the man's feet scratch the ground in pursuit. Andrew prayed for an out. With lightning-fast deliberation, he thought to turn and face the man alone, giving Renata a chance to make a break for it. Before deciding, he made out an L-shaped turn ahead. Another bullet screamed past them. They dashed around the corner. Streetlights glowed from an opening on the other side. They hurdled and dodged their way over more refuse. Andrew knocked over a stack of crates. The pursuer made the turn and hurried over the containers with ease. He set his feet. The primer clicked. Nothing stood between Andrew and Renata and the gun. Andrew's lungs tightened, and Renata dug her nails into his hand. They were mere steps from the opening when a second man stepped in front of them from the street. He had a revolver raised at Andrew and Renata. Andrew was so close to him that he could see the man's bared teeth as he pulled the trigger.

Andrew sank his chest to his knees and yanked Renata by the arm. They tumbled and slid across the ground as the shot whirred over them. Their pursuer from behind screeched in pain. He flung his gun, then fell to the ground, clutching his neck. Now lying on his back, Andrew looked up at the outstretched arm of his pursuer's accomplice, who had fired the shot. The man, realizing what he had done to his partner, froze just long enough for Andrew to reach up and grab his arm. The gun let off another shot. Andrew struggled to get to his feet, but the man forced him back to the ground. He tilted his gun towards Andrew. Andrew gripped the attacker's wrist and extended his arms, but the muscles and tendons violated by his knife wound faltered. The mouth of the barrel eased toward him, and its metal pressed against his cheek.

A shot rang out. A trail of bone and gray matter sprayed across the stone. The man's body tightened, then slumped. Andrew opened his eyes. His ears rang, and standing over him with two hands around the stock of a smoking revolver was Renata. Her chest heaved, and her nostrils flared with every breath. She glared at the dead man. Blood spilled like a faucet from his exit wound, just under the dislodged eye hanging by its optic nerve. The blood pooled toward Andrew. He slid the man off him and stood up. The acrid smell of gunpowder and chunks of spattered flesh on his lips made him cough and sputter. Renata lowered the weapon but could not move her eyes away from what she had wrought.

"Oh my God. Renata," Andrew said.

He waited for her heaving breath to ease and her frozen state to thaw. Renata turned towards him and took a shaky step. Andrew came to her, and she fell into his arms. He held her and waited until her breathing steadied before turning her face upwards at him. Her glazed eyes seemed to stare through him and into the sky, and she gripped Andrew like a lost child. She had done something dreadful.

"It's all right, it's all right," he repeated to her.

Horrid coughing came from down the alleyway. Andrew and Renata whipped their heads around and saw the feet of their wounded pursuer sticking out amongst some rubbish. He was lying on his back, his head propped against some sandbags. Blood seeped between his teeth. He stuffed his fingers into his jugular as red spilled from it. The pair approached him. Andrew reached to peel the gun from Renata's hands, but she tightened her grip. Stepping forward, she aimed the gun between the man's eyes and fired. His head kicked, then rested. Renata lowered the weapon. They watched the death rattle suffer before quieting. For a second, Andrew was entranced by the surreality of it. It was not until a raindrop struck his nose that his senses returned. He looked up—more followed. He turned to Renata. She stood frigid, with a grimace. Andrew reached down and eased the revolver from her hand. He slid it into his jetted pocket and laced his fingers into the same hand.

"Come on. We need to go," Andrew said.

Chapter 12

The rain came hard and strong, slapping the cobble-stones. Their cabby stopped a few blocks north of Ezra's place, near Parque Lezama. The driver refused to enter La Boca. Andrew paid him. He and Renata then dashed toward the safehouse. Andrew had the lapels of his peacoat up past his jawbone; Renata kept her shawl down. He offered his coat, but she refused. She daubed at the rain landing on her arms and seemed to have forgotten Andrew was there. She continued this peculiar cleansing for the next quarter of an hour, until they arrived. Renata knocked on the door.

"*¿Ezra?*" she said after several bangs upon the door. The pouring rain made it challenging to hear. "*¿Ezra?*" She struck the door again. No answer. She rummaged through her pockets, withdrew a key, unlatched the door, and stepped inside. Renata locked the door. The rain drummed the corrugated roof above. Renata rested her forehead against the wall and closed her eyes. She remained there for several minutes. Water dripped from her dress, sounding a steady patter against the floor.

"*Diccionario,*" she said.

Andrew withdrew the little book, and found, to his surprise, the layered wool had kept it rather dry. Renata flipped through its pages:

Dame—Give me
Tu—Your
Ropa—Clothes
Para—For
Que—That
Secarse—Dry (Itself)

"Okay," said Andrew. "Do you want me to—"

Without further instruction, she took a lantern, lit it, and directed him down to the basement. It was narrow, dingy, and frigid. Haphazard shelves held several jars of canned fruits and vegetables and medical supplies. Renata set the lantern on a high stool and fixed a clothesline on a nail from one end of the room to the other. She turned to Andrew and motioned for him to disrobe. Andrew slipped off his coat, followed by Papá's shirt. He bent over, unlaced his boots, and rolled off his socks. He peeled off his shirt, revealing a defined set of muscles from years of seafaring and farm work. The bandage held fast to his arm, bearing faint streaks of pink. Renata pinned each article with a clothespin and laid a run of rags beneath the line to catch the drips. She turned around and gestured toward his pants.

"What?" Andrew asked.

"*Pantalones,*" she replied.

"You want me to take off my pants?"

"*Sí.*"

"I can keep these on; they're fine."

She shook her head. "*No, te vas a enfermar.*"

"I will be fine." *Enfermar* sounded like the word "infirmary" to him.

"*No discutas conmigo. Hace lo que te digo.*"

He exhaled with a defeated groan. "All right, if you say so."

Andrew hooked his thumbs beneath the waistbands of his

trousers and underwear and pulled downward.

"*¡¿Qué cazzo?!*" Renata cried. She caught a glimpse of his nether region and spun around, shielding her eyes. All the blood in her body seemed to swell against her face. "*¡¿Qué estás haciendo?!*" she said with her back facing him.

"What? What?!" Andrew replied, hoisting up his pants. "I am taking them off like you asked me to."

"*¡Dije solo tus pantalones, no todo!*" she shouted emphatically.

"I don't know what you are saying. You know I don't," he replied.

She turned to look at him and grabbed just the waistband of his trousers. "*Solo esto; nada más.*"

"All right, all right," he replied, slipping off his trousers and revealing a pair of long-legged underpants.

She snatched the pants before the legs had left his foot and pinned them to the clothesline. She then pulled a blanket from the shelf and handed it to him.

"Go, *por las escaleras,*" she ordered, pointing him towards the staircase. Andrew raised an eyebrow and looked at her.

"But, what about you?"

She placed her pinched fingers against her chest. "*¿En serio? Tengo que cambiarme,*" she replied. Andrew felt the anxiety ooze from her.

"All right, I hear ya," he said. He wrapped the blanket over his shoulders and headed up the stairs. He shuffled to the dim kitchen and sat down on one of the chairs at the table. The lights flickering from the basement swatted at the darkness. He shut his eyes until he heard the staircase creak. She was no longer in her long, soaked dress but in a thin powder blue shaded chemise and an off-color nightgown—garment stock for the absconded women. Loose braids hung down the sides of her neck, and her Italian face was pallid and cold. She stopped and looked at Andrew in the light of the lantern. Neither said anything.

She approached the stove and kindled the firebox. She then lifted the *pava,* or kettle, from it, went to the door, and placed it just outside. As the fire blazed up, she went to the pantry and retrieved a tall jar and a chubby calabash gourd that had a metal frame affixed to it that extended into a tripod. She set these items next to the lantern, returned to the front door, and opened it ajar. The Argentine watched the *pava* plink and fill. When it had filled with rain to her liking, she brought it in and placed it on the stove. It hissed and sizzled as droplets slid onto the cast-iron surface. Taking the jar from the table, she dumped a blend of dried, chopped herbs, or *yerba,* into the gourd. She tilted it onto its side and shook it, covering the top to prevent spillage. When the kettle began to steam, she took it off and poured the hot water into the gourd. The water swirled into the grassy substance. She filled it until a tiny shore of *yerba* sat on the surface. Her preparations were completed when Renata plunged a metal straw fixed with a perforated bulb at the end, called a *bombilla,* into the gourd.

She took a sip. Judging by her pinched face, Andrew thought she did not care for it. Renata took another sip, poured an extra dram of water from the *pava,* and tested it again. Her tongue smacked as it studied the flavors. She nodded, then handed it to Andrew. Andrew looked at her and pointed at himself.

"*Sí, toma,*" she said. Her voice sounded aged.

Andrew pressed his palms against the gourd's warm skin and nipped from the bombilla. He put up his nose; the earthy, steaming residuals of what he thought tasted like tree bark slithered down his throat. He forced a smile and took another sip. This time, it pleased him. Past the loamy infusion were organic fragrances with a sumptuous, tea-like bite. Renata urged him to finish it, and so he did. He handed the gourd back and gave a thumbs-up.

"*¿Te gusta?*" she asked.

"*Sí.*" He coughed from the near-scalding temperature of it.

"*Se llama maté.*"

"*¿Mah-teh?*"

"*Eso.*" She nodded.

"I noticed some fellas having some when I arrived. I was wondering what that was."

For a while, they shared the maté in silence with placid contentment. They passed it back and forth each time Renata provided the refill. It was pleasant and for a moment strengthened their sensibilities. The bombilla throttled, and Andrew slid the empty gourd back to Renata. As she wrapped her hands around it, her lip started to tremble, and so did the rest. Her eyes swelled. She tried to resist the emotion but soon gave way to unrestrained sobbing. Andrew came to her side, and she fell on his chest, wailing. Her body seemed to melt with grief and horror, and Andrew held her to keep her from falling out of her chair.

She wept until she could weep no more. Her throat tightened, and she started to sputter and sniffle. Andrew cradled her in his arms.

"Let's get you to bed," he said.

He managed to lace a finger through the handle of the lantern and carried her like an infant to the basement. His foot pushed on one of the doors of the adjacent rooms. It was at most ten feet long and four feet wide, with a stained mattress placed in the middle. A mirror and a crucifix were nailed to the walls, and a *mezuzah* was fixed to the door frame. He laid her gently on the bed, then from another room retrieved a few spare, shabby blankets and a pillow. He covered her with the blankets and slid the pillow beneath her head. Her sniffling eased. He sat over her, in a chair next to the mattress, with the blanket she'd given him still over his bare shoulders. He began to nod off. Renata slid out from the sheets and sat up. The movement startled Andrew; he straightened his drooping head and looked at her. Her bleary eyes gleamed in the reflected lantern light. She looked around at her accommodations. She stretched her arms out and yawned. Then, turning her eyes to Andrew, she said in a fluttering voice, *"Vení."* Andrew, unaware of the command to come in Spanish, said nothing and continued to look at her.

"Vení acá, conmigo," she said, reaching for him.

Andrew watched her touch him. With a tug at his fingertips, he complied. He lifted the sheets open and entered beneath them. She was still a bit damp, and so was he. Her hand patted the space behind her. Andrew crawled over her and laid himself along her back. She scooted into him and nestled her backside into his pelvis. Andrew kept his hand by his side, but Renata took it and brought it against her chest. His elbow slid over the convex groove of her waist, and his fingers felt the outlines of her breasts beneath the saturated chemise. His heart thumped. Renata shuffled her head closer to his, pressing wet hair against his face. Andrew reared back.

"Perdoname," she apologized softly. Renata rose to pull her hair away, but Andrew kept her still.

"It's all right. I got it," he said. Andrew took her hair and squeezed the strands together, then set it over her shoulder along the side of her neck.

"Gracias," she whispered, taking it from him.

Andrew returned his hand to her chest, and she held it close. Her thumb drifted over his weathered knuckles until the sweet warmth carried them to slumber.

Chapter 13

"Get up," said Ezra. His foot nudged Andrew's side. Andrew grumbled and showed him his back. "Up, I says."

Andrew peered up to see Ezra standing over him. His eyelids pulled back. "Hey," he said. Andrew did not know what to say.

Next to him lay Renata, content and eyes closed.

"Wake up her," said Ezra.

Andrew placed his hand on Renata's shoulder and nudged her awake. She pinched her face, stretched her arms, and yawned. She turned to look at Andrew but noticed Ezra first.

"*¡Ezra!*" she said, clutching the sheets to her neck.

"*¡Vestite!*" he said, tossing her dress at her. His teeth clenched, and his lips snarled.

"*Ezra, escúchame, no es culp——*"

"*¡Te dije que te vistas! ¡Ya está! ¿Entendés? ¡Se terminó!*"

He was yelling at her. Renata looked on in dread. Her chin started to tremble.

"*¿Qué?*" she asked in a shuddering voice.

Ezra did not hold back. In Spanish, he covered the litany of infractions they had committed last night. Worse, he listed what the ruffians knew: her name, her family, her home, and even the church Renata's family attended Mass. He added that the ruffians likely knew the location of the safehouse they were in. He laid the blame on Renata and the sailor's *imprudente* behavior. When Ezra told Renata that she could no longer work for him, tears formed in her eyes. She begged and pleaded her case, but Ezra would not hear it. All the while, Andrew watched in stunned silence. When he saw Renata falling apart, he shot up from the bed and wrenched Ezra by the shirt.

"Stop it! What's the matter with you?!" he shouted. Ezra tried to throw him off, but his skeletal arms had little effect against Andrew's weight and size. Andrew slammed him against the wall, causing Ezra's glasses to slip from his face. "You listen to me, and you listen good," Andrew snarled. "She's been in for one hell of a night. The last thing she needs is this. If you had let us stay here in the first place, none of this would've ever happened."

"It doesn't matter now, *yanqui*," said Ezra. "She exposed. They knew you both! Now, she lost. She no good to help here now. Now, she no longer safe. And what she to you, sailor-man? A whore to bed."

Andrew socked Ezra in the face. His head jolted. Renata clasped her hands over her mouth.

"Andrew, stop!" she cried.

"Say it again! I dare you, you sonuvabitch!" boomed Andrew.

Ezra tasted the blood coming from the edge of his mouth and chuckled.

"I've known worse, *yanqui*," he said. "When you do and see what I do, nothing is scare."

"You sure about that? Awfully brave for someone who picks on ladies." Andrew tightened his grasp.

"This change nothing! She can't work for the cause anymore; she is too compromise now."

"She has given everything for you—for this, and you're just going to throw her to the wind?" Andrew asked.

"What's it to you? Your ship leave in the hour," Ezra said, lifting his pocketwatch. It was five after six; Captain O'Kelly had scheduled *Dismal Queen's* departure for seven. "You be gone, and she to be here without you. What then do you do? Nothing! You Americans come break stuff and go like nothing. Then, go, *yanqui*! Go and break stuff elsewhere!" Andrew loosened his grip on Ezra's shirt. Ezra pushed himself away and glared at them both. "Both of you, make dressed and get out!" Ezra stormed upstairs. Andrew turned around and looked at Renata. Her chin had steadied, but her cheeks bore tear streaks.

"I'll—I'll get changed in the other room," said Andrew. Renata, still holding the covers over herself, nodded.

Andrew's clothes were no longer soaked but not entirely dry. It did not matter; he knew he needed to get back to *Dismal Queen* soon. Once dressed, he left the basement. Ezra was in the kitchen with a rag pressed against his swollen lip. He glanced at Andrew and said nothing. The squeak of Renata's feet climbing the staircase sounded. Ezra beelined for the door and unlocked it.

"*Afuera,*" he said.

Renata looked for his eyes, but Ezra refused to give them. She tightened her bottom lip and walked out. Andrew fixed his cap on his head and followed her. A zephyr swam between the conventillos of La Boca. The barrio was its usual self again: the sun and clouds above, and locals ambling to work with tools and lunch pails in hand, the bumpy streets shining from yesterday's deluge—rinsed and distilled. The events from last night seemed like a dream. Renata kept her head down and proceeded northward. They did not speak. Andrew tried to think of the right thing to say while Renata brooded.

"*¿Vahs ah ah-sare?*" Andrew asked.

"*No lo sé*; I don't know," she admitted as she watched her feet graze over the stones. She eventually stopped and looked at Andrew with those eyes he loved. "*Pero voy a encontrar algo,*" she said reassuringly. Andrew managed a smile. He knew she would be all right, and so did she.

The sadness followed them and stung when the waters of Puerto Madero glistening in the sunlight came into view. There stood *Dismal Queen*. Her anchor chain clacked and rattled as her heavy fluke rose from the depths. Most of the crew were onboard and preparing the ship for departure. Andrew and Renata stopped within the shadow of the warehouse and peeked around.

"I think we're good," he said with a half-hearted grin. He turned to Renata and pulled out the dictionary. He read:

I—*Yo*

Need—*Necessito*

To—*A*

See—*Ver*

You—*Tú*

Again—*Otra vez*

She nodded and tucked her lips in. Andrew felt his throat shrink and pressed a finger into his eyelid to plug his tear duct.

"How?" Renata said. The timbre was feeble and filled with worry, yet full of tenderness and longing. Andrew felt his heart breaking inside. For all that he was and all that he knew, he wished not to go. A thought came over him. He glanced around the wharf and noticed a nearby foreman with a clipboard.

"Wait here," he said.

Andrew jogged toward the foreman. After he spoke with him

with the help of the dictionary, the man handed Andrew the pencil tucked behind his ear. Andrew returned to Renata and opened the inside back cover of the dictionary.

"*Me dir-reck-see-own;* my address," he said, showing Renata his scribblings. "Write to me when you're safe," he said. He pretended to write a letter out on his hand, then he pointed at himself and said:

I—*Yo*

"*Voy a*"

Find—*Encontrar*

"*Tu*"

Soon—*Pronto*

Renata nodded and wiped her eyes. Andrew handed her the dictionary, then held her tight. She wrapped her arms around his waist and squeezed. He brushed her hair and rested his chin against her crown. They stood like that for a while. He then placed a finger beneath her chin. She tilted her head up at him. Their eyes glistened. So much feeling and uncertainty swelled between them, and it reduced them to blithering laughter. Andrew leaned into her. Renata laced her fingers together around his neck, and they kissed. They kissed to remember as they did to forget; they kissed to know so they could dream; they kissed to believe that a kiss could do so.

Andrew stepped away and thumbed the tears from her eyes. "I'll be back," he assured her. Renata understood. Her hands fell from his. He waved goodbye and made for the ship. He bolted up the gangplank and to the edge and leaned upon the rail facing the port. He looked at Renata. Her hair fluttered in the breeze, and a break in the clouds made it seem like Heaven itself was shining upon her. She lifted her hand to shield her eyes from it and smiled.

"I'll be back! You'll see!" he shouted to her.

"Hey Andy," came a dreary voice behind Andrew.

Andrew spun his neck around and looked over his shoulder to see Vincent standing with two other sailors—their faces grim.

"Oh, hey, Vince," replied Andrew. He turned around and continued to wave at Renata, when something caught his eye. Barry and a couple of others from *Dismal Queen* were walking along the dike toward Renata. Before she could notice the approaching sailors, they had snatched her by the arms. Andrew felt his stomach drop to the floor.

"No! Stop! Stop! Renata!" he cried. As he whipped around to make for the gangplank, a sudden grasp of hands and arms around him stopped him in his tracks.

"What the—? Hey! Let me go!" Andrew shouted.

"This is for your own good, Andy," said Vincent.

Vincent had Andrew by the neck while the two other sailors held him by the arms. Other members of the crew started to gather around them—some with confused and others expectant stares.

"Vince, Vince! What are you doing?! Let me go!" said Andrew, gagging.

"Andy, calm down," he said. "We will be on our way shortly, and this whole thing will be behind us. Like you say: another place, another port. Yeah?"

Andrew struggled to pull them off, but their grip around him was firm and rigid. From the corner of his eyes, he saw Renata struggling in the hands of sailors, and Barry with them, conversing with a few men in dark suits. Andrew was held, paralyzed, as Barry and the others handed Renata over to the ruffians. He was consumed by fear, followed by rage. Andrew fought with all his might: kicking, punching, clawing, and throwing his body in every which way he could. The ship's sixth bell sounded as Barry and the other sailors jogged up the gangplank. He parted the crowd of shipmates looking on and headed straight for Andrew.

"Hold him steady," he shouted. Without missing a step, Barry threw his fist into Andrew's stomach. The force knocked the wind out of him, and he keeled over.

"Hey! Take it easy," said Vincent, finally letting go of Andrew's neck. Andrew gasped and coughed.

"Take it easy?!" repeated Barry. "You know what I told you. You know what he and that *porteña* did!"

"Barry," Andrew wheezed. He braced himself with one hand on the deck and the other massaging his throat. "What are you talking about?"

"Don't play me a fool, you sack of shit. It was you and that bitch who took the harlot from El Nacional. You, who started this whole mess. You were the one that beat that fella, and now they say they found two more dead this morning." The watching crew began to murmur. "I should have handed *you* over—but your little strumpet will do. I cut a deal with them kikes, and all it cost was her." With a wily grin, he turned around and announced to the others, "And I made good on that account, boys. We got the brothels back!"

The sailors whooped and hollered. Andrew's rage reached a boiling point, and an eerie sickness stewed in the pit of his stomach—every ounce of his being wanted to kill Barry. All seemed lost until he noticed a dense weight tugging downward on his coat: the revolver Renata used last night was still in his pocket. Andrew ripped his arm from his handler and reached into his coat.

"Back! Everybody get back!" he shouted. Andrew spun

around, brandishing the weapon at everyone around him; the sailors ducked and backed out of the way of its iron sights. Andrew scooted toward the railing and looked over. The gangplank was gone. The white water churned beneath the ship. He looked ashore for Renata. The ruffians had her splayed out like hide on a drying rack, holding her by arms and feet. Passing dockworkers and policemen stepped aside and turned their eyes down, pretending not to notice Renata's cries for help. She continued to scream and thrash about until one of the ruffians yanked her by the hair and struck her across the jaw. Her body went limp.

"Put the piece down!" shouted Barry. "You ain't got it in you."

Andrew pointed the gun at him. Barry sneered. Andrew slid his finger against the cold trigger guard. The foghorn sounded, and *Dismal Queen* oscillated away from the harbor's edge.

"Come on, Andrew. It's not worth it," pleaded Vincent.

"Listen to your betty," said Barry. "It's done."

The entire crew—including Captain O'Kelly and his staff from the bridge—watched in horror as those nearest Andrew begged him to disarm. Andrew looked back at Renata. Two of the ruffians carried her by the shoulders, with her feet bumping along the ground. He leaned over the edge and peered down. The ship was a few meters from the dike's edge. He believed he could survive the drop if he managed to keep his senses and keep clear of the ship's undercurrent and propellers. What remained was to decide if, indeed, his heart was onshore in the hands of the ruffians.

Andrew straddled the rail, the crew edged nearer, the ship drifted farther, and blood coursed through his veins.

Chapter 14

"Dinner!" chimed Abu's voice.

My mind transported itself back to the present. I sat hunched over the book on the coffee table with my nose inches from its pages. I looked up towards the kitchen. As I did, I noticed my grandfather. He had been awake for some time, I reckoned. Beneath his gray whiskers, he wore a smirk, and there was a twinkle in his eye. Before one of the hundreds of questions I had could leap from my mouth, my grandmother entered the room.

"I made empanadas," she announced. A steamy trail of vapors followed the golden-crusted, meat-filled pies on the plate in her hand. She set it on the coffee table and handed me one wrapped in a napkin and another to her husband. His rolled sleeve slid down his forearm as he lifted the empanada to his mouth, revealing a scar from a wound many years ago.

"*Gracias, mi amor,*" he said to her. The old man took a bite and started to fumble with the burning piece in his mouth.

"*Tené paciencia,* you beast," she said with a giggle.

"You know I can't help myself. *Me encanta demasiado tu comida,*" he replied. Abu smiled and leaned into him for a kiss. Grandpa turned towards me.

"Well, go on," he said. "Tell us how it is."

My dumbfounded expression surely did not go unnoticed as the pair looked at me with wry grins. I came to my senses and took a bite. The smooth crackle of the crust, followed by a rush of hearty, meat-filled flavors, was just as delightful as I had read. I nodded with approval.

"You can search far and wide, but you'll never find empanadas as good as your *abuela's.*"

I gave a facile smile and gazed at the two of them. Abu stood next to Grandpa, with her hand on his shoulder.

"Grandpa," I said, picking up the book and holding it by the spine. "Is this … were you … what happened next?"

My grandpa's cheeks swelled. He turned to his wife, looked into her hazel eyes that he so loved, and, with a steady warmth, said, "Well, I suppose you could say he followed his heart."

About the Author

Follow Nicholas Warack on social media and stay updated with further content and updates!

You can connect with me on:
- https://twitter.com/nicholas_warack
- https://www.facebook.com/nwarack
- https://www.instagram.com/nicholaswarack
- https://www.tiktok.com/@n.warack